# FORBIDDEN BABY

LEXIE MIERS

**1**

———

*D*AVID.

*I have no idea where this relationship is going, but damn does she have a nice ass.*

My cock throbs inside my jeans as Jenika wriggles her hips while navigating the tables of the restaurant. She throws me a smile over her shoulder as she ducks into the ladies room and the waiter arrives with our dessert.

"Thanks." I wave away the lingering waiter and stare down at the cheesecake I ordered under sufferance.

Jenika loves dessert, an adorable, yet annoying tendency. Aggravating because it delays our bedtime and that was the best time of day.

A smile tugged at my lips and I fiddled with the fork. I'd never looked forward to going to bed with a woman so much.

I chuckle to myself as I think about the weird and wonderful life I now have.

I spend my days inventing new football boots, trading information with other scientists, and running my billion dollar company. I get to run around the best football fields in the world and I get treated like a god because people value money and power over all else.

Yet, now, my favourite time of the day is when my red-haired vixen slips off her dress and reveals her body to me.

Jenika re-enters the room in a ray of sunshine and smiles, and once again, I feel my lips lift and a grin stretch across my face as happiness fills me. After a decade of dealing with gold digging bitches, I was pretty sure I'd found one I could trust, and spend quality time with.

"That looks yum," Jenika said as she sat down with a big, beautiful smile on her face and picked up her spoon.

She cracked the burnt sugar crust of her crème brulee and moaned as she scooped the custard into her mouth.

Heat poured into my groin and I glared playfully at her. "You've gotta stop making those noises or I'm going to pull you into the car and take you home. Dessert or no dessert."

She laughed. "You know I have to eat my calories now. I'll need them for energy later."

I chuckled and winked at her. "True. We still haven't tried the shower out yet."

"That's because you're impatient." She sighed as she continued to eat.

"Again. So, true."

I let my gaze wander over her loving the way color blossomed in her cheeks as I stared suggestively at her.

She was such a strange combination of innocence and intense sexuality. She'd only had a few guys before me. Fellow university students mostly. I hadn't asked, because I didn't want to know, but they must have been pretty crap in bed. Because the moment I took her into my arms and kissed her, she'd melted like ice in summer. She was enthusiastic to learn what I liked and to share new experiences with me.

I'd never had a lover like her. Her enthusiasm, her honesty, her affection—it was all new and intoxicating.

When I saw the spoon enter her mouth for the last time, my patience dissipated.

"Let's go, gorgeous."

I hadn't touched my unwanted dessert but she'd consumed hers in a few mouthfuls.

She swallowed and gave me a big smile. "Okay."

I stood and grabbed her hand. She jumped to her feet also and I pulled her into my arms. "Bed time."

She giggled as I threw my credit card at the manager, and then got her out of the restaurant and into the waiting limo. I shut the door with a bang.

Jenika slid to the other side of the long bench seat and gestured to the vast amount of room around her. "I don't know why you always insist on this car. I feel like I'm going to my debutante ball, or something."

My driver started the limo and pulled into the heavy San Francisco traffic.

"You know I like having my hands free to grope you all the way home."

She slipped a hand over my hip and grabbed my thigh with her small hand.

"I missed you this week, you know?"

I grabbed her around the waist and pulled her onto my lap, inhaling her spicy scent.

"I've been busy, babe. You know I wish I could see you more." I had my seventh pair of football boots coming out in a few weeks, and my first line of soccer boots. Work was crazy at the moment.

She leaned forward and kissed my lips lightly, the softness as sweet as it was teasing. "Yeah, I know, and I'm proud of all the work you do. You're amazing. I just wish I saw you more, that's all."

For once, I didn't hear any pressure in her tone, just sadness.

"Come here." I pulled her closer, loving the way her arms slid around my neck and she held me tight. Like she'd never let me go.

I pressed my lips to hers and slid my tongue into her mouth. Tasting her sweetness and loving the little moans that rose from her throat the longer we kissed.

When things got hot and heavy I pulled back, not wanting to be fully erect for the long elevator ride up to my penthouse. We'd been caught far too many times by my neighbours already.

"How was your week?" I asked, glancing outside to see how far we had to go.

"Good." She smiled. "The new principal is a bit of a dick, but hey, I can handle it."

Jenika had graduated from university last year with a double degree in commerce and finance. But amazingly she'd decided to go into teaching, and work with some pretty tough kids.

She was resilient and kind, and I had squashed the urge to slide in and help her with her career. She should be teaching at a good school, or at a college level.

But I hadn't and she was happy. When she succeeded on her own chosen path, I wanted her to know that it was because she'd done it entirely on her own. There was a lot of satisfaction in that. I should know.

"I know you can. You're one tough girl."

"I'm twenty-three, David."

Oh, the impudence of the young. "And baby, I was travelling around Europe making my first million while you were still in nappies."

"I was not! There's only fifteen years between us!"

That was so true, but I loved teasing her about our age difference.

The limo slowed and I looked outside, the footman from my building already opening the door for us.

"Let's go, baby."

I slid across the seat, stepped out and offered her my hand. She gave me one of her playful glares.

"When I start calling you Daddy, you're not going to think it's so funny."

I laughed as I pulled her from the limo, a part of me rather turned on by the obscenity of that kink.

"You didn't tell me you were into role playing. Wanna try that sometime?"

She shook her head and her mouth turned downward. I mentally kicked myself for forgetting her father issues. We hadn't talked a lot about our families or our pasts, but I did know that her father hadn't been in her life for long.

"Are you sure?" I continued to joke, putting my arm around her shoulders and guiding her inside. "Any other kinks you want to try? BDSM? I'm not so good with ropes and handcuffs, but for you, I'd try anything."

She giggled as I placed a hand on my heart, swearing to be any lover she wanted.

"I know, but what we do now is more than enough," she whispered as she slid her hands around my waist and gave me her come-hither look.

The elevator dinged and I managed to get her into the lift and up to my penthouse without stripping her out of her sexy black dress. Which was incredible considering how I was feeling.

My heart was beginning to pound like a drum that I could hear inside my head, and my hands were wandering on their own accord, feeling her beautiful soft curves beneath her dress.

"I want you." I groaned as I pulled her to the bedroom, our lips stuck together, our hands pulling and tugging at each other's clothes.

She managed to get my shirt open and my suit pants undone before I'd found the flesh I wanted.

"Wait a sec," I said, stepping back from her groping hands to push the shirt from my shoulders. "Strip. Now. I can never get that dress of yours off fast enough."

Despite my constant offers to buy her new clothes, she always refused. Choosing to wear the same dress a dozen times.

She gave me a beautiful slow smile, then stepped back and gave a little shimmy of her hips, the black dress sliding to the ground with practised ease.

She stood before me in black lacy underwear.

*Now, they're new!*

"Damn, you're sexy."

She gave me a small smile. "I have spent more money on my underwear in the month I've known you, than the ten years before it."

I pulled at my tie and shucked off my pants. I'd offered to buy her as much lacy confectionary as she desired as well. But again, she's always refused.

Now that I knew how amazing she looked in it, I was going to steal some, write down the sizes, and order everything that Victoria's Secret had in her size.

"And I appreciate it. You know I'm a sucker for the window dressing."

She smiled and stepped forward, wrapping her hand around my shaft.

"I do. I do…"

She worked her hand up and down me exactly as I liked, her smile turning devilish as the blood began to pound and his cock began to thicken for her.

"Come here, beautiful girl."

I cupped her face and devoured her mouth. Loving the passionate way she kissed me back. The way her tongue lifted to meet mine, and the small moans she uttered as I stroked her skin with my fingertips.

I reached behind her and undid her black lacey bra, letting it fall away between us.

I trailed my lips over her cheek and bit down on the side of her neck. She arched into me, her hands running over my hips and grabbing my ass.

She bit my butt one night, which gave me the biggest shock. But was also a major turn on. I never knew what was going to happen with Jenika, and that alone, made my heart race in anticipation of these nights.

"Shower?" she asked, panting a little.

*Good girl. I would have forgotten completely.*

"Oh, absolutely."

I took her hand and we walked into my massive en suite. I'd had this apartment built specifically with a huge double shower, for this exact purpose.

Jenika grabbed the tiny black piece of lace between her legs and pushed them down her legs and onto the floor. Then she stood back up and I got to view her, in all her perfection.

"Yum."

I picked her up and put her on top of the bench, spreading her legs and pressing between them. She wrapped her arms around my neck and kissed me, letting her hands wander over my shoulders, setting my body alight.

I dropped to the tiled floor and set my mouth to her bare pussy.

"Oh… fuck," she cried as I let my tongue circle the tiny little pink bud between her thighs.

She smelled like rain and sunshine. Fresh, clean woman. And it was intoxicating. I couldn't get enough.

I ran my tongue up and down her folds, loving the little screams she made as she grabbed my hair and panted for me to stop. To go on. She didn't seem to know what she wanted.

I kissed her clit one more time before moving back up to standing once again, giving both of her perfect rose- colored nipples a good suck on the way up.

I kissed her lips softly this time, her eyes wide and dreamy.

"That was amazing," she said, swaying a little where she stood.

"Well, let's finish it shall we?"

I grabbed her hand, tugged her into the shower, so aroused my balls were tight and aching.

I turned on the water, adjusted it until it was hot enough to cause steam to swirl around us in a white mist.

"Come here." I pulled her into my arms and pressed her back against the grey tiled wall. She gasped and arched her back to get away from the coldness, so I turned the double heads to encase us both in strong, hot jets of water.

She moaned as the heat flowed over us and I lifted her up and pressed her against the wall with my body, her legs naturally going around my waist.

"Ah, oh…" She gasped and I captured her mouth with mine as I lined up the head of my cock with her open body. I bent my knees and pressed my cock into her waiting and willing pussy.

"Ah fuck!" I groaned out.

I needed to be fully inside her. I slid right into the hilt and clenched my hand into a fist beneath her ass to give myself some control.

I so wanted to cum. Right now. My balls ached and my will power flew straight out the window.

Jenika writhed against me and I clamped down in restraint. She needed me, and I wasn't going to let her down.

I pulled back from her, and then thrust back in. She groaned and I kissed her neck. I slid back into the warm depths of her body and rolled my hips.

I loved the focus of my body at this one moment, the lack of thoughts in my head. Jenika always captured my attention, one hundred per cent.

I transferred her weight slightly and took both ass cheeks in my hand, driving into her over and over in an increasingly fast rate.

She clung to me, her nails digging into my shoulders as I sunk deeper and deeper.

Her eyes flew open and she caught my gaze, staring deep into my eyes. Her mouth was open, water streaming down her neck. Her hair plastered to her face.

I'd never seen a more beautiful sight. Ever.

"I… I…"

I moved faster, waiting for the telltale sign that she was about to cum on me.

Her pussy gripped me tight and I knew this was it. She cried out and her eyes slid closed as she began to convulse, her greedy pussy milking me for all it was worth.

Heat tickled up my hamstrings and my orgasm flooded through me with more intensity than a storm.

My cock pulsed inside her and she cried out again, surprised.

I pulled out as fast as I could, belatedly remembering that she still wasn't on the pill.

I flooded the shower tiles with my cum, groaning out my release as she cradled my jaw and kissed me with all the passion that she had inside of her.

Slowly our breathing, that was once ragged and full of gasps, changed. Blissful sleepiness flowed over us both.

She unhooked her legs and I let her slide to the floor, stepping away and beneath the continual spray of heat.

"Wow, gorgeous."

She staggered to the twin shower head, appearing like a drunkard on a Sunday morning. "That was…. incredible. I so have to go on the pill. I know you said I don't have to but…"

I shook my head, cursing myself for my lack of foresight. I thought I'd be able to control myself as I had with all the others, but I couldn't. This had happened a few times now. We were lucky nothing had eventuated from it.

"I was wrong. I have no control with you. That would be great, thank you."

She smiled her dopey, post-climax smile. "Okay, I'll make an appointment with my doctor next week."

I turned off the showers and grabbed some towels for us, wrapping the bath sheet around her perfectly voluptuous body.

She had more flesh than most of my exes. Her breasts were bigger, her ass big enough to fill both hands. And I loved it. She was all woman.

"Let's go to bed, baby."

She fluttered her eyes lashes at me. "Yes, Daddy."

I chuckled out a startled laugh and corralled her into my bedroom and beneath the sheets of my king-sized bed.

"Okay, okay. Does *gorgeous* work for you instead?"

"Perfectly," she said as she smothered a yawn. "What are you up to tomorrow night?" She settled into my arms like she'd always been there.

Jenika was one of the only women I've let stay in my bed for a full night. I've struggled with insomnia for many years and found a body next to me, disturbing to say the least. But on the few nights she'd stayed so far, I'd actually slept better than usual.

A habit, I was not in the mood to break. A good night's sleep was sacred.

"Ah, early meetings. Family shit tomorrow night." I kissed her cheek and let my body settle into the mattress. "Why?"

"Oh, just wondering. You don't talk much about your family."

There was a reason for that. Like most people, my childhood had been *shite*.

"Not much to tell. My dad's the only one left and our relationship isn't exactly stellar."

She hummed in agreement, her breathing getting quieter as she began to fall into sleep.

"What about you? Weekend plans?" I asked.

We'd only had a total of about a dozen dates over the past few months. I didn't know much about her either.

"Yeah. Um…. family wedding tomorrow night and then some function on Sunday too. Maybe we could have dinner again on Sunday night, David? Unless you wanna wait until next week?"

My Sunday nights were generally filled with research and set up for the week ahead, but another night of this could never be a bad thing.

"Can I let you know on Sunday? I can't commit to anything yet."

She laughed and snuggled closer. "Yeah I know. The downside of dating a workaholic."

I kissed the back of her neck. She wasn't the first woman to wish I didn't work so much, but I was pretty sure her motives were sweeter than theirs.

"You mean a billionaire." I corrected her.

The perfect curve of her shoulder moved up and down in a shrug. "Whatever."

I rolled my eyes, though she couldn't see it.

"You are the *only* woman I've ever dated who didn't love that title."

She twisted around and looked up at me so that her brown eyes were open and I could see the honesty of the words that would come. "David. I love that you're intelligent and hard-working, and the money and lifestyle you have is awesome. But I'd still want you if you managed a restaurant, or were a chef or something."

"But then I wouldn't be me," I argued. My success and business skills were an integral part of who I was.

She kissed me gently on the lips and tilted her hips in invitation once again.

"You'd be you. I just wish I had a way of showing you that I love you for more than your money. If we'd met at college…or something like that."

Her eyes widened as she realised what she'd said.

*I'd still love you…*

The usual panic that would happen when a woman would use those words on me didn't arrive, which was surprising.

I asked, with more confidence than I felt. "You love me, huh?"

She bit her lip. "I'm starting to. I think."

I wasn't going into that conversation any deeper, so I pressed her onto her back and rolled on top of her lush body to re-aquaint myself with its beauty.

"Well, when I invent a time machine I'll go back and meet you as a nobody. See if you like me just as me."

She gasped as I pressed deep. "I guarantee that I would."

## 2

*J*ENIKA.

"Mum. I seriously can't believe you want to get married again. Aren't two divorces enough?" I asked as I grimaced at the abomination staring back at me from the mirror.

*Whoever said lavender was a good wedding color, was as blind as a mole.*

"No. And this time, it'll stick, Jenika. I'm sure of it."

My mother sat at the dressing table, handing pins to the hair-dresser as she arranged my mother's artificial curls into a pretty creation on top of her head.

"And why is that, Mum?"

My mother had been married twice since I was born. My father, who'd run away before I'd started school. He'd been a lawyer, or something she said.

And my stepfather, who'd been so mean that I'd asked to go to a boarding school when I was fifteen, and never went home again. He'd only lasted a few years after that, and by then I was at college.

My mother did not have good taste in men.

"Because he's rich!" my mother said as she swiveled around in her chair, her heavily made-up face alight with happiness.

*Well, that explains why we're in this ridiculously expensive hotel for the wedding.*

I rolled my eyes. "Mum! Is that it? Seriously?"

I looked away, my cheeks hot with anger and shame. How had I come from a woman like this? Sure, I loved her, the best I could, but we were so different it was embarrassing to think we shared genetic make-up.

My mother stood up and walked over to the mirrors, dismissing the hairdresser and makeup artist from the room.

"It isn't just that, sweetheart. He's a nice man. We get along well. And with you all grown up, and me getting older...I don't want to be alone."

My anger dissipated as I heard the truth in her words and our eyes met in a moment of understanding.

I gathered her gently in for a hug so I didn't crush our outfits, then turned back to the mirror. There stood a bride, in a stunning gold and white skirt suit. And me. The truly, ugly bridesmaid.

I took a deep breath, pushing my torrid parent-hating feelings down and away.

"Well, then I wish you all the happiness in the world, Mum, we all deserve it. Including you."

She reached over and squeezed my hand. "You do too, Jenny." Her nickname for me that I had hated my whole life. *Yuck.* "I hope you aren't going to be married to your job forever."

I smiled and opened my mouth to share my news with her. That I indeed would not be married to a demanding job for long. That I had a boyfriend, and he was everything I wanted in this world.

"Actually, Mum..."

The door to the bridal suite opened and Maree, one of my mum's oldest friends popped her head in.

"They're ready for you, Sue."

Mum took a deep breath and smoothed her skirt down with her hand. Her slight shiver was the only betrayal of the nervousness she obviously felt.

"Alright, let's go."

Mum went to move away and I grabbed her back for a moment, upset with myself for having such negative feelings towards her on this day of all days. I stared into brown eyes that were a mirror image of my own.

"I really hope this works out for you, Mum. I love you."

She raised her hand and cupped my cheek for a minute and I let out a long sigh. We had a strained relationship at the best of times, but surely, both being adults now, we could work towards a better one.

"I love you too, my daughter. Now, let's get this show on the road."

I laughed, clearing out the clogged tears in my throat.

"Okay. Let's do it."

I was yet to meet my mother's new beau, but I had my fingers crossed that for once, she may have picked a nice man.

I grabbed my little bouquet of white roses and walked through the door in my uncomfortable shoes.

The pretty hotel chapel held only a few dozen people, but as the traditional Wedding March played softly on the piano, I walked down the short aisle with my head held high. If this was a new beginning for my mother, then I would support her the best I could.

The man at the end of the aisle had a kind face, a balding head and a round belly. I met his gaze, his face seeming familiar in a strange way.

He smiled at me and I returned the look, my belly flipping over as I tried to remember where I'd seen him before?

If he was that wealthy, maybe I'd seen him in a magazine somewhere?

I shuffled to the left side and turned around to watch my mother walking down the aisle. Her smile was radiant and my heart was full of worry for her.

But she was a big girl and I'd promised myself when I was fifteen and leaving home that I wouldn't stress about her anymore. I took a breath and pushed away the worry.

She arrived at the top of the aisle, handed me her flowers and turned to hold hands with the man in the centre.

I balanced the two bouquets awkwardly and lifted my head once again. My gaze shifted to the left of the couple and my eyes met a pair of bright blue eyes that were far too familiar.

My shock was mirrored right back at me as David stared at me from across the aisle.

"Dearly beloved. We are gathered here today to join together Jack Turner and Sue Grange in holy matrimony."

I gasped and jumped back, my heart pounding like a racehorse on the final leg of a race.

*Oh, my fucking God... that's David's father, marrying my mother. And that will make him my...*

I stared at him, my future stepbrother, my mouth agape, tears gathering in my eyes.

He stepped behind his father's large form and I couldn't see his eyes anymore.

I followed his example, hot tears clogging my vision and probably smudging my makeup. I gulped in air, panic swirling in my mind.

What the hell were we going to do now? How could we continue with our relationship if he was my stepbrother? What would people think? How would we explain this?

I took a few more calming breaths, ignoring the worried looks my Mum's friends were throwing me.

Did it really matter? It wasn't like we grew up together or anything. Just because our parents were married, didn't mean...

*It's not like we knew this was going to happen.*

My stomach tightened painfully, acid burning in my throat making me want to vomit up the little I'd had for breakfast.

The short, surprisingly sweet ceremony finished after the traditional vows and the exchanging of rings. The newly married couple turned toward the small crowd and began walking down the aisle together.

That left me facing the very well dressed, best man.

I stepped forward, anxiety tightening my chest as David offered me his arm, as the best man to the maid of honour. I had no choice. I wobbled forward and took the support he offered.

He didn't look at me as we walked behind our parents and I shook all over.

*What on earth are we going to do now?*

I let go of his arm as we moved into the next room where the reception was being held. I hurried over to the bridal table and got caught by my mother.

"Jenika, I want you to meet my new husband, Jack. Jack this is my only daughter, Jenika."

The man in front of me, that I could now see resembled David, smiled kindly at me as the band struck up the first chord of music.

"Lovely to meet you, young lady. I'm sorry it took this long for us to meet."

I shook his hand and felt the hairs on my neck prickle up as David stepped closer.

"Thank you, sir. I wish we'd met earlier too."

He grinned and pulled David into his side. "Well, we're family now, so there's no getting away from me."

I tried to laugh but it was so strained I saw David's eyes roll as he met my gaze.

"Jenika, Sue, this is my son David. He's a brilliant scientist and owns the world's largest football boot company."

"Oh, he sounds just like a chip off the old block then, Jack." Mum laughed and I cringed as David's gaze hardened.

He'd always professed to be a self-made billionaire. Maybe he'd lied about that and just spent his family's money to get even wealthier?

David's lips tightened into a grimace. "I made my fortune on my own. My father's wealth and success has nothing to do with mine."

Jack chuckled with good nature. "That's true. He practically disowned me in college, saved his money, took his designs and flew to Europe. Came back a millionaire. And that was ten years ago now."

The pride in his father's words and expression were too obvious, and it hurt me to see it.

*Lies, lies, lies.* David had always said that his relationship with his father was strained— bad even. Why would he be dishonest about something like that? To keep me out, and stop me getting too close?

*What else was he hiding?*

"Are you married, David?" I asked, crossing my fingers mentally that some skinny blonde wasn't about to materialise with a string of kids in tow.

Jack laughed. "Married to his job, my boy is."

David's blue eyes were as cold as stone marble and his mouth twisted up.

"Oh, so is she!" Mum laughed as though we were the funniest comedians in the world. "Looks like we have even more in common than we thought, Jack!"

The two of them walked off together to sit down in the prime positions for the day, chatting happily about how similar their children were.

David and I took our seats at opposite ends of the bridal table and my phone vibrated in my handbag. I went to grab it and my mother slapped my hands.

"Don't you dare grab your phone again, Jenny. You promised."

My gaze slid over to where David was tucking his cell phone back into his suit jacket pocket. The message had to be from him. Well, he'd just have to wait until later.

"Fine, Mum. Sorry."

I managed to go through the motions and eventually became numb to the shock of it all. We smiled at the photographer, got through the lovely dinner they served, and stood up with our parents for the first dance.

*Now let's see what he has to say for himself.*

As we swayed on the small dance floor to some soppy music my mother had picked out, David danced us far enough away to have our first true words of the evening.

"Did you know about this?"

The words were practically hissed at me and my stomach plummeted at the sight of this angry side of him.

"Me?" I yelled at him and our parents looked over at us with worried expressions. I smiled at them and then plastered an even faker smile on my face for David and anyone who watched us. "Me? Are you fucking kidding me, David? I have never been so surprised in my whole life."

His lips thinned out and he had an ugly look on his face that I hadn't seen before, and couldn't really decipher.

I frowned at him. "Why are you looking so angry with me? What did I do?"

"I've met your mother before. A couple of weeks ago, but I didn't know she was related to you. You have different last names."

*Why does that sound like an accusation?*

I glared at him. "Yeah, and? I have my father's last name and she still has my stepfather's name. What's your problem?"

"My problem," he hissed through his teeth, "is the fact that I feel like I've been fooled by a couple of scam artists. Was this the plan all along? To snag two rich husbands? Because I can tell, baby, you failed where your mother succeeded. You know that you were nowhere near that goal."

If he'd hit me, I would have been less surprised.

I pulled out of his arms and marched off to the bathroom, pushing open the door to the ladies and letting loose the feral scream that had been building.

"Argh! You fucking… asshole!"

Mum's friend, Maree, ran into the bathroom after me, her face a mask of worry and strain. "Dear, what on earth is wrong?"

Tears streamed down my face and I couldn't stop them. I choked on my words but even though I would have loved to confide in a woman I'd known since I was a child, I knew I couldn't explain it to her.

"I…I…"

Maree searched through her clutch bag and came up with a wad of tissues for me, and I wiped at my face. My makeup was going to be an absolute disaster.

*Sorry, Mum. At least the photos have already been taken.*

"I heard Jack's son is a bit of bastard, dear. He has quite the reputation. I hope he wasn't too horrible to you. You don't get that rich and popular without knowing how to throw people off buildings when you need to."

*I know but he's not always like that...*

"No, it's just..." My throat was full of tears, hot and heavy. Like someone had their hands wrapped around my trachea.

I shook my head, giving up on any hope of communicating. I went over to the large bevelled mirror and dabbed at my red face with cool water and the tissues

*Damn you look like a mess.*

I couldn't go out there looking like this.

"The wedding's almost over anyway, dear. Another hour or so and you can go home."

I nodded again and forced myself to take several deep breaths. He was just in shock. Surely? The David I knew, the beautiful, thoughtful, loving David I knew, would not be accusing me of being a deceitful bitch. Surely, he knew me better than that?

A sinking feeling filled me and the hope that he would realise he was mistaken, sunk like a lead balloon.

I'd been judged on my mother's merits before. The boys at school assumed I would be as easy with them, as my mother obviously was with the older men.

The girls boarding school that I had attended after that was the best salvation I could possibly come up with. And it had worked. I'd come a long way since my days as a bullied teenager at a tiny high school in the sticks.

"Thanks, Maree. You're right. You go back and enjoy the party. I think I'll just sit here for a bit. Okay?"

She patted me on the shoulder and I waited until she'd left the room until I let out the massive sigh building in my chest. I sunk down onto the faded pink couch in the corner of the room and lay my head down.

Surely the night couldn't get any worse than this?

**3**

AVID.

*I've NEVER been this angry. Ever.*

And that was saying something considering the mountains I've had to climb to get where I was today. The narcissistic personality types I've had to conquer. Men and women combined. They'd all wanted my money, and I thought I'd gotten pretty good at spotting a gold digger from a mile away.

I was getting rusty.

"What did you do to that girl, son?" my father asked, having pulled me aside after Jenika ran from the room a moment ago.

*Stupid girl. You could have held it together a bit longer.*

"Nothing."

"Bullshit."

I rolled my eyes at his language. Seriously? Like that was going to get me to open up and explain?

"Dad. I better go. Got heaps of work to do tomorrow, and I'm sure you can do without me now."

He backed off a little. His eyebrows rising on his forehead. "I was a bit surprised you turned up at all. Actually."

So was I. But I'd tried to do the right thing, and look what I got for it.

"Well, I wanted to meet the gold digger's family…oh I mean, your wife's family."

My father glared at me and I stared blankly back. He had no power over me anymore. I had stopped needing his approval a long time ago.

"Don't say that, David."

*Don't tell me you've fooled yourself into thinking this woman actually cares about you?*

"Why? It's true and you know it, Dad. You've known her barely three months, she doesn't have a cent to her name, and you're twenty years older than she is. You're telling me she married you for your good looks?"

My father's chubby face grew more and more purple.

I waited. Part of me thinking that he's going to hit me out of spite, and I know if that happens, I won't defend myself.

Anything to distract me from the sickening pounding of my heart will be a good thing. I still couldn't believe what had happened tonight. My world had completely twisted on its head.

*The betrayal! And I didn't see it coming!*

"Get out of here, David. Now."

I falter. Pardon me? "I'll see you later in the week, for lunch yeah?"

We have a lunch catch up every Wednesday. Some weeks I am so busy I go to cancel, but my promise always catches up with me. To spare one hour a week for the man who raised me. My executive assistant reminds me every Tuesday.

My father finally nodded. "Yes, I'll be there. I have something to talk to you about. A joint family venture between Sue's and mine, and I want your help."

"My help?" That would be a first.

My father was calm now and that scared me. What had he thought up to bind this new woman to us even more than she already was?

"All right Dad. See you on Wednesday."

Dad went back to his wife, a woman who had accomplished something that a hundred before her hadn't: gotten my dad down the aisle

He'd had a long procession of girlfriends since my mum died. So long ago I didn't even remember her. But none of them had stuck around very long.

The only consistent women in my life had been my aged German nanny, and my assistant, Rose, who was as smart as a whip, and as gay as blazes.

I looked over to where my seventy-year-old father held the woman he'd just joined his life with.

Maybe something was different about this one? Or maybe Dad was just scared to die alone?

Either way, I hoped he had a solid pre-nup and an ironclad will. Not that I needed the money. But I'd rather it go to a charity, or cancer research, then *her.*

Jenika stepped back into the room, lifting the front of her strapless purple gown awkwardly, the stupid thing didn't fit her properly.

Why her mother put her into a dress like that I'd never know. Jenika had the curviest hips and the perkiest breasts. If I'd given her a black sheet to wrap around herself, she would have looked ten times better in it, than that horrendous thing.

She looked my way and our gazes met, a hundred small moments we'd shared flashing through my mind.

The anger rose, as did the pain. I was out of here.

I grabbed my jacket, relieved to be free of my duties. I walked across the dance floor, past the woman I would have called my girl-friend last night, and strode straight out into the balmy summer night.

Of all the things I could have learnt tonight, the fact that my gorgeous, honest girl had pulled the wool over my eyes, would have been the last thing I'd have put money on.

*Ah well. There were always more fish in the sea.*


WEDNESDAY AT LUNCHTIME, I sat at our normal table, waiting for Dad to arrive. I could only imagine what he'd come up with for this supposed 'family venture.' He really was getting odd in his old age.

"Hi son."

"Hey Dad."

We greeted each other with a smile and a handshake, and Dad sat down.

"How's your week been, David?"

*Frustrating as fuck.*

Jenika had called me three times on Sunday and left a few messages asking for a chat, or at least an explanation for my anger, but I couldn't give it to her.

I'd poured all my frustrating into testing my new soccer shoes, and as a result my knees were killing me.

She hadn't messaged or called since, and although I knew I should be relieved, there was a coldness in my gut that would not go away. It resembled the grief for my mother I'd carried for far too long.

So, I reached for a half truth. "Not bad. New soccer boots are coming along well. How about you? How does it feel to married again after almost thirty years?"

My father's old face lit up like fireworks on the fourth of July.

"It's great actually. I'd forgotten how nice it was to wake up with the same woman every day."

"I wouldn't know." I spat out at him.

*And I like it that way.*

But despite my instant reaction, my father's appearance gave me pause. He was glowing in a healthy, vibrant way that I knew had nothing to do with good sex. I'd seen the women who had passed through my dad's bedroom when I was a teenager, and they were so much more beautiful than Jenika's mother.

So what did this woman do to make my father so happy?

There was a part of me that was envious of him. He was happy. A place I was very far from. Especially since I'd found out what Jenika was.

I still couldn't believe I had been *that* wrong about her.

"No you wouldn't, which is bloody obvious. How do those sour grapes taste, David?"

"Like crap."

My father laughed wholeheartedly and called the waitress over so we could order.

After ordering his usual meal, my father put both of his hands on the table in front of him. His once bare fingers were now carrying the heavy weight of a thick wedding band and it smacked me hard to see it.

"I want you to know that I've altered my will to include Sue."

*I knew it. I wonder how much Jenika gets out of this deal?*

"Of course. It's your money, Dad."

"All of your inheritance still stands as is, and you know I've given forty per cent away to your mother's breast cancer charity."

"Yes."

I was waiting for the punch line. Surely, she'd wrangled herself a good deal?

"So, what is your new wife getting then?"

"I want to buy her a home so that she'll be looked after when I die. I've put aside a little bit of maintenance money, but nothing special. It's a home she really needs."

That didn't sound too ominous, unless he was talking about a twenty-millionaire dollar apartment in New York?

"Alright, so what does she want? A penthouse apartment?"

He shook his head. "Oh no. Sue and I want to move further out of the city. About two hours drive we've decided would be our limit. And we've already found a nice house on a hundred hectares and I think we could be happy there. Relaxed. Away from everything."

"You're selling your house?"

*My family home?*

"No, of course not. That house is yours. I've had the papers drawn up and I'm going to transfer it into your name. I know how much you love that house."

Shock flooded through me, wiping all other thoughts from my mind.

"I don't know what to say, Dad."

And I didn't. Did the man who had disappointed me so many times in my life, really know what I wanted now?

"Look, I know I haven't always been there for you. Losing your mother when you were so young, I didn't cope as I should. But I am intensely proud of you, and want you to know that I care."

My nose tingled and my throat ached from the tears threatening my composure.

I nodded and reached for my glass of water, swallowing it down.

"Thank you. I don't think I'd move in now though."

I liked my apartment, and my family home was exactly that, a house that should be filled with a family. Which I was not.

"No, I doubted that. But since Sue and I will be taking any staff who wish to move with us, we'll close the house until you're ready to move in. It's a perfect family home, for lots of kids. It was why your mother asked me to buy it for her. She always envisaged lots of children running up and down the halls."

*But she never lived long enough to see it.*

"Alright. Thanks, Dad."

I didn't know what else to say. My strange childhood and serious abandonment issues, if my psychiatrist was to be believed, meant I had no plans to ever marry or have children. But I appreciated the sentiment, and the fact that his new wife would never get her hands on *my* mother's house.

"So, what did you need from me then?" I asked, as our lunches arrived. Steak sandwich for my dad, and the big breakfast for me today.

"I want you to go out to the property we've chosen and find out if it's worth buying."

*That's an odd request.*

"Isn't that something you should do?"

"Well, yes and no. I'm not interested in massive drives and you know building, and real estate better than I do."

That was true, but somehow I knew there was a catch, and I hadn't smelt it out yet.

"I suppose I could drive over for a visit for you, if you really need me to."

"I do. I want your opinion. On everything, because we want you to visit. I know every Wednesday might be out of the question, but tell me if it's somewhere you'd consider coming every month for a weekend. A family retreat."

I narrowed my eyes at him.

"What's the catch, Dad?"

He held up his hands and waved them. "No catch. Sue and I want your opinion. If you're never going to visit us and it's too far away from the world, then we'll choose another location."

There was something fishy about this, but I'd bite for the moment.

"Alright. Well, a break might be in order, I've been slugging my guts out a bit hard lately. Would this weekend suit the realtor do you think?"

A beaming smile spread over my father's face and I was glad I'd managed to make him happy.

"I'm sure I can arrange it. It's still fully furnished although the owners haven't lived there for over a year. They're hoping to sell it all as a package and just walk away. The real estate agent said you can stay a few days if you like."

"That might not be a bad idea."

*Get away from work, breathe some fresh air.*

Escape the ghost of Jenika that seemed to be lingering around my apartment and in my bed.

"Brilliant. I'll let the owners know and I'll ask Sue to tee up where you can pick up Jenika."

*What the fuck?*

"Pardon me?"

Had I heard that correctly?

"Sue has asked Jenika if she'll do the same thing, of course. We only have one child each and we want you both to be happy. You're family now, after all."

*Yeah, well the problem is that I've fucked this so called family already...*

"Dad, I can't. It's really out of the question."

His eyebrows lowered and his eyes narrowed. "Why? I really don't understand why you've taken such an intense dislike to her. Her mother says she's lovely."

*Yeah, lovely, and conniving, and far too good at playing sweet...*

"She's a schoolteacher for god's sakes, Dad. What do I have in common with some sweet schoolteacher from goodness knows where?"

"Oh, stop being such a snob. Not everyone was made for science. Now, this is my one condition to you getting the house, my boy. I don't ask you for much, but I am asking you for this one thing. Take Jenika with you; try, for my sakes to make peace with the fact that you have a stepsister now. I know you don't play well with others."

"Don't treat me like a child, Dad."

"Then don't act like one." He snapped back and I clenched my teeth as rage poured through me.

If Dad knew I'd already had the sweet little teacher on all fours, begging for my cock, he'd think very differently about his new stepdaughter.

"Dad…"

My father held up his hand and I stopped the vitriol that was about to spill from my lips. This was not something I would be able to take back once out in the open. Sue didn't seem to have told him yet, and it wasn't the one who would expose everything.

"If you want the house, my house, David, you will do this one thing for me. You will take your new sister to the house I want to buy for my new wife, and you will both decide if it's a home you would visit. Spend some time together, bond. I don't care how you do it, but if you want what I have you'll do this one thing for me."

My Dad took a wad of papers out of his jacket pocket and placed them down onto the table.

It was the deed to my parent's home. A house I would not allow to fall into this new step mother's grasp.

And as I met my father's eye, I knew he knew it too.

"Alright, Dad, you win. I'll take 'Jenny' to this house you want to buy and we'll give you an honest appraisal about its future possibilities. But don't be surprised if we both say we wouldn't visit. You know I rarely leave the city for anything other than work."

"I know. I'll send you the details, where to pick Jenika up, and all that."

He finished his sandwich and threw some greenbacks down onto the table.

"See you next week, son. I look forward to hearing what you think."

He patted me on the shoulder in a condescending way, but left the deed on the table.

I waited until he had gone and then picked it up.

He'd already signed it over to me.

*Fuck Dad!*

I groaned and wanted to throw my hands in the air. He had me there.

I wanted this house a lot more than I wanted to stay away from Jenika.

I picked up the papers and held them in my hands, weighing them as though the few flimsy pieces of paper could contain the house they represented.

Hopefully this country estate was as good as my father thought it was. Because if Jenika and I could lie convincingly, we could move our parents off to the country and not have to deal with each other ever again.

**4**

---

*J*ENIKA.

"Your Dad wants us to do what?" I practically yelled down the phone, my heart pounding so hard I could barely hear my own voice over the drumming in my ears.

I'd been waiting for days for this call, and the last thing I expected from David was a business proposal.

"My dad said your mum was going to organise this with you, but I hadn't heard back from either one of them, and since we're meant to leave tomorrow, I figured I'd just call myself."

I rolled my eyes. "My mother doesn't tell me anything. I didn't even know she was getting married until two days before the wedding."

There was silence as David digested that information, then he continued.

"Well, anyway. Dad wants to buy an estate in Napa Valley for your mother and him and he wants us to go check it out and see if we like it too, since supposedly we'll be going down there and spending time as a...family."

He practically spat out the last word and I cringed. Where was all this hostility coming from?

"Just tell him we can't go. I have reports due in a week. I have to work all weekend."

Another long silence as I waited for David to respond.

"He's asked me, as a personal favour. And it's for the weekend. We leave on Friday night."

I bit my lip and held my breath. Not sure how to answer that. I didn't want to spend a whole weekend with David. Not unless he was going to actually talk to me. He was so angry, and I still wasn't sure what I'd done wrong. Other than be related to a woman I'd never been proud to be connected to.

"David, I really need to talk to you about what happened on Saturday, and us."

*I thought we had a future. I told you I loved you. What happened?*

"There is no *us*, Jenika. We're related now, in a really sick way. I think we should just focus on trying to get along while we can, and see if we can get through a weekend together. This property allegedly has some sort of fruit orchard attached to it, and when I called Dad he said you had experience with that sort of industry. Or something."

*So, my mum actually remembered some of my adolescence? Amazing.*

"Yes. I did fruit picking, and estate management on the holidays through high school and college."

"I see."

*I really don't think you do.*

I desperately wanted to tell David everything, and beg for a second chance with whatever he thought I'd done wrong. But I didn't. I couldn't get the words out.

*And if he wanted to hear my side of the story, he would have answered my call on Sunday.*

"So, what time do we leave tomorrow?" I asked.

I really didn't want to go, but I could hear from his tone that we had no choice.

"I'll pick you up from work and we'll drive straight there. It's only about an hour and a half and we're expected to stay for the weekend. So, organise a bag, alright?"

He sounded so efficient, so business like and cold. I hated it, and it gave me the strength to respond back the same way.

"Fine. See you then."

And I hung up.

Mobile phones didn't give you the same satisfaction when hanging up on a person that they did when I was little. When you could slam the received into the cradle with an almighty crash.

Now, you had to push a button with a single finger with gusto. It really wasn't as satisfying.

So, I had to wait until tomorrow to see him, my lover, and then I had a weekend in Napa Valley with him. Just lovely, our first holiday together and it was as brother and sister.

*Vomit.*

FRIDAY.

After a hellish day with struggling teenagers, I was ready for a relaxing weekend amongst the fruit trees. I loved my job, I truly did, but working in a school with low socioeconomic kids was a tough gig every day.

I saw a black sports car pull up to the curve.

*Who would be in this neighbourhood with that sort of car?*

The horn beeped and I jumped. Could the driver be any more rude? Who was he waiting for? I stared at the dark tinted window as it rolled down.

"Get in, Jenika." David's annoyed voice barked at me through the opening.

"Oh!" I jumped up and grabbed my roller bag, walking towards the flashy looking Porsche.

I pulled open the door, threw my bag in at my feet and hopped in. I sat on the seat with my feet resting on the bag, feeling awkward and young.

I'd never asked him what his car was. The only time he'd ever picked me up was in a chauffeur driven town car or the limo.

"I didn't recognise you in this car. Sorry."

He grunted and pulled into the traffic.

*Great. I made him mad already and we haven't even gone anywhere.*

"How was your week?" I asked him and he shrugged his massive shoulders.

"The new boots doing well?"

"Yeah."

Great conversationalist. Fine. I didn't need to chat.

I pulled out my phone and fell into the world of Facebook, a place I'd never included him, so was safe and carefree.

Over an hour of looking at people's photos, doing some reading and sending some messages to friends, and we still hadn't spoken.

David's knuckles were white at the wheel and I heaved out a sigh as I finally put my phone away and glanced out the window. We should be there soon, surely? It felt like we'd been driving for days and I hadn't seen a house in ages.

"I think this is it."

David pulled over beside a sign that said, "Hillside estate."

"Not the most original name." I commented, not impressed with the sign, nor the lack of life that surrounded the house that I still couldn't see.

David shrugged. "I don't care about the name. As long as the house is good enough for our parents to get away, that will be great."

He turned the car back on and we headed down the winding road. We threaded through the apple and peach orchards and happiness warmed my chest as memories filled my mind.

"What are you smiling at?" David asked.

"Oh, just memories. I loved working on the fruit orchards as a teen. It was bloody hard work, but the people were great, and the food was amazing."

I risked a glance over to my ex-lover and he was frowning, that thick muscle in his jaw flickering as he clenched it.

"Seriously David. You've gotta tell me what on earth is going on with you."

He turned to glare at me. "Seriously, Jenika. I don't."

He got out of the car and slammed the door.

*Whoa. You need to start talking about what's bugging you before you explode.*

I followed suit and grabbed my bag. When I got out of the car the house before me took my breath away.

"Wow."

I stared up at the country mansion, with its massive columns and planted flower beds. I couldn't imagine a more picturesque home for my mother to grow old in.

"What else did you expect? With my father's money I knew it would be huge."

I opened my mouth to explain that I had no bloody idea how much money his father had but David had already trudged up the stairs.

I exhaled slowly and tried to let go of the anger that was beginning to swirl in my gut. I had done absolutely nothing wrong, and this misunderstanding had gone on long enough.

I grabbed my bad and ran up the stairs after him.

He'd opened an envelope, taken out keys and was unlocking the front door as I stepped up next to him.

"Looks like we have the house to ourselves for two days, but there will be a woman arriving with food tomorrow. Hopefully someone delivers all the way out here so we don't starve for dinner."

I shrugged at him and pushed past him to get inside.

There was a dusty, slightly stale smell to the air, but the décor was just amazing. Beautiful fabrics, warm carpets. All done in neutral tones with a hint of peach.

"I'm going to look around."

I dumped my bag at the foot of the curving stair case and took off around the house.

The living room was lovely and when I found the kitchen I sighed with sheer happiness. There was a massive six burner stove top and traditional fittings around the wooden country kitchen. This would be the best place to bake, especially in winter.

The room unfortunately also had a stale smell to it, so I unlocked the back door, allowing some fresh air in.

David, the storm cloud, trudged into the kitchen and crossed his arms over his chest.

"I think I'll open the windows, it smells really funky in here."

David nodded. "Yeah, I agree. I'd thought that our parents had already come up here and seen it, but from the way things are, I'm going to assume no one's been here for months."

"I wonder why it hasn't sold. It's beautiful."

"Money probably. The price tag is very steep."

I ignored his comment about money again and danced off into the dining room and then up the stairs.

If there were no bedrooms downstairs, that may be a problem long-term, when Jack or my mother couldn't climb steps any longer. Although installing a lift would probably fix that.

I wandered down the carpeted hallways and stared at the paintings on the wall. This place had a lovely warm, family feeling to it.

And if it was me, I'd love to spend my days roaming these halls and cooking in the kitchen. But I'm sure that was the last thing David wanted to hear.

*Yeah, imagine if I started talking about houses and babies. He'd run away from here screaming.*

A giggle escaped my lips as I walked into the master bedroom. The huge four poster bed was one to marvel over.

"What's so funny?" David's dark voice said behind me.

I jumped and whirled around. "Damn it, you scared me."

His eyebrows had lowered once again, as though he was determined to be grouchy no matter what. This wasn't a side of him that I'd seen before, but I was sure I could pull back the David I knew.

"It wasn't really funny, more as just happy. This house is amazing, so warm, and non-modern. I love it."

He nodded and watched as I walked over to the en suite.

*Spoke too soon.*

"Bathroom is old and dusty, and peach… bleh. But look at that spa bath!" I stared at the awesome, dated bathroom and sighed. "I think I'll make this bed with clean sheets, clean the bathroom and have a bath."

I garnered my confidence and turned to face him.

"Wanna join me?"

There was a chink in his armour as pain slashed across his face.

"You know we can't do that, Jenika."

"Why? You still haven't given me a reason to why you, so hastily ended out relationship."

He rolled his eyes and I gave him my best death stare.

"Seriously David, what is your problem? Did I scare you when I told you that I loved you? Was that it? Because you didn't seem to have too much of a problem with me when I was in your bed last Friday."

That got a reaction. His eyes grew dark and stormy and he charged towards me.

"You know I still want you, I can't help that. But we're related now, and I don't trust you! I cannot date someone I don't trust."

"What are you talking about? I am the same person I was a week ago, a month ago. A teacher who loves her students, and who is madly in love with your stubborn ass!"

"Don't say that. You know we can't be together."

He was so close, I could touch him, and I couldn't stop myself. I reached out and cupped his face in my hands, drawing him closer.

"David, please. Don't give up on us. I'm still the same person, and I can prove it to you if you'll give me the chance."

His hands came up to my waist and he pulled me in tightly against his hard frame.

A moan left my lips as my pussy clenched with longing and my knees went weak.

"You've got the weekend to prove me wrong, Jenika. Because if you can't, I'll be moving on as soon as possible."

"I'll take that deal." I grinned up at him. *This was going to be easy.* "Kiss me."

He dove on me like a starving man. His tongue spearing my lips as I gripped his shoulders hard, lest I fall.

Our clothes fell to the floor in a tumble of tugging and shedding. My heart raced as my hands found David's hot skin. His chest hair curling beneath my palms as we got naked.

I turned and stripped the dusty covers from the bed, finding clean sheets beneath.

We fell onto the soft bed and I pushed David until he was lying on his back. I wanted to kiss him and love him until he realised that I wasn't anything like my mother. That nothing had changed between us.

I slid down his body and took him into my mouth. The salty, warm taste of his thickening cock on my tongue as I moved on him in that way that he'd taught me.

His fingers tangled in my hair as I moved up and down.

"Come here," he said and I slid up his body to kiss him.

Our lips connected and his hand went between my legs, teasing the flesh and sliding a finger inside me.

I gasped and groaned, digging my nails into his shoulders and pressing myself as close to him as I could get.

This couldn't be over, yet. It just couldn't. We had too much between us. Too many possibilities and futures before us.

I threw my leg over his body and pushed back so that his cock lay against the aching flesh between my legs. I'd never known these feelings before I met him, but now, I didn't want to live without them.

"I need you, David." I moaned and his hands came up and cupped my breasts. Stroking the nipples and tweaking the flesh before moving down and positioning himself underneath me.

The head of his cock pressed against my slick folds and I tilted my hips back and slid down onto him.

We both groaned in unison as I took him inside my body, one inch at a time.

David grabbed my hips and began thrusting, not letting me take control at all.

He pumped up into me hard and I grabbed onto his strong forearms and let the feelings overwhelm me.

With each thrust of his hips, the heat would flow through me. Pushing me higher and higher, up that mountain of orgasm.

"Oh. Fuck…oh…"

Feral noises left my throat.

My insides tightened as David grunted and moved beneath me.

I began to come. Pulses of pleasure moving through my belly and lightning shooting down my thighs.

David pulled out just as he squirted, white liquid pulsing all over his belly as I collapsed onto him.

Kissing him, gripping him hard.

He rolled away from me and got up.

"I'll just get cleaned up, hang on."

He got up and moved into the en suite and I looked down at the glistening wetness on my chest. I needed a shower too.

I moved into the bathroom and waited for him to finish his shower.

"No room in there for two, huh?"

He smiled at me but didn't respond and I could feel the distance between us still.

"You want to grab some dinner and then go to bed?" I asked.

He nodded. "Yeah, I'm pretty hungry."

He stepped out of the shower, grabbed a worn towel from the bench and wiped himself down.

I jumped in and turned the hot water on, determined to stay positive and happy.

"I'll go see what they have, and if there's a pizza place, I'll get it delivered."

"Thank you."

He headed off and I was left wondering what I could possibly do to convince him that I was nothing like my mother.

I washed my hair, and put on some comfortable clothes.

We'd have some dinner and head to bed. And no matter what, I was making sure we slept here together and he got to remember how much he liked sleeping next to me.

Surely that would fix everything?

I heard the doorbell peel and David called out, "Dinner's here."

I trotted down the stairs to the smell of cheesy pizza and gave him my biggest smile.

"Awesome. Can't wait."

We ate quickly and I dragged David to bed pretty soon after that. I knew I had a long way to go, but our relationship was worth fighting for.

**5**

─────────

$\mathcal{D}$AVID.

Sunlight was streaming in through the ugly peach curtains and I blinked rapidly awake. Where was I again?

*Oh right. Dad's new love nest.*

I look down and there's Jenika, still snuggled against my chest, her long hair spilling over her shoulders and touching my arm.

*Damn, she's beautiful.*

*And too clever – like her mother.*

The foul thought made my lips twist into a grimace. Could I really be in a relationship with a woman I didn't trust? The short answer of course, was no. But how could I get that trust back?

Jenika snuggled her butt back into my groin and my cock leapt at the invitation.

*No. Not again.*

I needed some air, some space to breathe. I'd always found Jenika too sexy, too irresistible. And when she was my girlfriend that was fine. Who wouldn't want a woman in their bed they couldn't keep their hands off?

But now that attraction was going to cloud my judgement, and I needed all my wits about me if I was going to come up with the right conclusion.

I disengaged my arm from her hip and rolled away.

My nose tickled from the dust.

*We better get a cleaner in her today or I'm not going to be able to assess this house properly.*

I picked up my clothes and pulled them on; they were still lying on the floor where I'd thrown them last night.

Memories of the sex we shared flooded my mind.

*Bloody vixen...damn she's hot.*

I shook my head to clear the red hot images and stole a glance at the bed where Jenika had rolled onto her back. Smudges of perfect pink nipples peeked above the sheet line and something inside me softened. I wanted to be closer to her again.

*No!*

I turned and trudged out of the bedroom, determination filling me as I jogged down the stairs and looked for my phone.

There was a list of contacts in the kitchen and I needed to get onto them.

A basket of fresh, delicious looking food sat on the kitchen bench. Fruit, pastries, a bottle of juice.

How had I missed someone coming into the house with this?

What time was it? I picked up my cell and almost dropped it again.

*10am!*

Since when had I slept this late? Not since I was a teenager.

*Amazing.*

I opened the basket and pulled out a croissant, biting into the buttery pastry while perusing the list left by whoever had brought the food.

A cleaner! That was where I needed to start.

I made a phone call, organised for the woman to come within the hour, and retired to the library with the accounts for the property.

Jenika found me half way through the books, wrapped only in a sheet and a beautiful smile on her face.

"What are you doing?"

"Looking over the figures to work out if the property is worth buying."

She walked around the desk and pushed me back so she could slide into my lap.

"Jenika…" I protested, but she did it anyway.

*Sucker!*

"Show me. Do they sell their produce for a profit? Or are you talking about making enough money to cover the general running of the house?"

She seemed to be thinking about our goal and her tone was sharp. I pulled the ledger towards her.

"Have a look. I'm hoping some of the records are on a computer somewhere, because this old system is a pain in the ass."

I leaned back to get away from the soft skin I longed to touch, and she shuffled forward to stare down at the numbers.

"So, what do you think, oh stepsister?"

Jenika cringed, as she always did when I mentioned our new relationship status, and I the tingles of guilt shot through me.

She slid off my lap and walked around the desk and sat in the chair opposite me.

"It depends. Does your dad want to make money from this venture? Or is he just looking to pay the bills? What should I be looking for?"

"How much do you know about business management?"

"I minored in business management. I'm qualified to teach accounting at a high school level, legal studies as well."

"Aren't you a bag of surprises?"

She shrugged. "You never really wanted to know about my past, or my schooling really. You focused on the present, and that was fine with me."

The accurate assessment surprised me and I found myself taking another look at the woman in front of me and once again saw all the beautiful aspects that had drawn me to her in the first place.

"You don't look much like your mum."

She huffed out a weird laugh. "Oh, I am nothing like my mother, or my father… I hope. Mum tells me he was smart, a lawyer I think, her stories always change. Anyway, I've tried very hard not to fail at the same things my mother has."

"Like what?"

"Like schooling, jobs, relationships."

"Marriages?"

She glared at me. "Yeah, well, I haven't had any of those."

"So… you're not close?" I asked, unable to help getting drawn into a conversation I didn't want.

"No. I told you that months ago." She sighed, her shoulders dropping from their defensive position. "My stepfather was a bit of a prick and I left home. Mum and I have tried to mend the rift between us, but we're pretty different."

I swallowed hard, all of my assumptions about Jenika coming in to bite me, hard.

"So, you didn't know your mother was marrying my dad?"

She rolled her eyes. "Hardly. She sprung it on me a couple of days before, handed me that god-awful dress, and cried until I agreed to stand in as her maid of honour. We aren't exactly close, but she did feed me for half my life. I do owe her something."

I didn't know what to make of any of this, and wasn't sure which line to take.

Jenika lifted her head and my eyes couldn't resist hers…as always

"David, I am not a gold digger, nowhere near it. I know you have money and I don't care about that. I never have. Did my mother marry your dad because he had money? Partly yes. Would I do the same thing if I was fifty and alone? Not a chance. But I don't expect to be divorced and lonely in my old age either. So, I suppose…I don't know."

She rubbed her forehead and looked away, her distress catching.

"Okay, look, let's just forget about it for a bit, okay? Let's concentrate on the estate, and we can leave all our personal stuff for later."

She took a breath, her lush cleavage deepening and her breasts swelling over the tops of her singlet.

"Okay. Let me have a look at those numbers again."

I pushed the books at her and waited for over twenty minutes while she scanned the accounts.

Finally she sat back with a smile. "It looks like these guys are actually turning a profit."

"Yeah, that's the conclusion I came to as well."

I gripped the chair arms tightly in my hands so I couldn't reach over the desk and touch her face. Bare of artifice or makeup. She wasn't even wearing earrings.

"But do our parents really want to be running an orchard? How many staff do they have?"

"I need to do a bit of digging, but from what the realtor said on the phone, the couple who own this house haven't lived here for years. It's pretty self sustainable."

Jenika's face lit up like a child on Christmas morning.

"That's great. At their age they really shouldn't be picking fruit for anything more than their own appetites."

The doorbell rang and I took the opportunity to stand, though my cock ached and my hands itched to rip the sheet off her and bend her over the mahogany desk.

"That'll be the cleaner, so you better go put some clothes on."

I tapped her on the ass and ignored her huff of disappointment—or whatever it was—as I made my way to the front door and let in a team of three women.

I introduced myself and they soon set about cleaning the house from top to bottom.

I took the basket of food out onto the patio and sat in a wicker lounge.

The soft sunlight filtered through the trees around me as I mulled over the situation, hoping to find a fly in the ointment, somewhere. But as I breathed in the peach-scented fresh air and watched the woman in the kitchen briskly cleaning away, I couldn't think of a reason my father shouldn't spend his time here.

It would be great for his high blood pressure and hopefully his new wife would encourage him to take walks around the property. It could add years to his life.

"So, what are you thinking?" Jenika grabbed for a pear and bit into it, laughing as juice dribbled down her chin Oh, food! I'm starving."

. Her hair was tied back in a ponytail, and she wore basic jeans and a black tank top. Accentuating how beautiful, fresh and young she was.

I yearned for more of her, and the hatred grew like a weed.

"I think we both know how we feel about the place. We should head home after lunch."

I stood and dusted off my jeans, though there was nothing to brush off.

Her eyebrows rose comically high. "Oh, why? I'd love to stay another day. Just to look around. I never get out of the city, and I don't think you do either."

She was right there.

"What are we going to do then? Other than go through more of the finances, which I'd be interested in looking at. But that won't take a whole day."

In fact, I was pretty certain this was a great investment for my Dad's latter years. He would enjoy the slower pace and the healthier lifestyle.

I wasn't sure how many times a year I could bring myself to drive out here, but hey… lying to him about that wouldn't be a problem.

Jenika gestured to the fruit trees. "We could start with a walk around the orchards maybe? See how healthy they are," she suggested and I couldn't think of a fast enough excuse to say no.

"Sure."

She grinned and grabbed a croissant. "Shall we?"

I chugged the last of my orange juice from the glass bottle and placed it down, before I followed her into the fresh air.

The sun warmed my skin and my muscles relaxed. The atmosphere out here was so different to the city. My body was humming to a different music.

"Isn't this incredible?" Jenika practically sang as she skipped around the orchard, the dappled light playing over her face.

*Yes. Yes it is.*

I kept walking and when I was relaxed enough to ask her the question that needed to be asked, I opened my mouth and got it out.

"I have to say, I find it really hard to believe that you didn't know that your mother was marrying my father."

Jenika groaned and threw her hands up in the air. "I've already told you I didn't know. I rarely see my mother."

That was interesting. "Why?"

"Honestly? Because she wasn't a good mother, and we have nothing in common. I left home at fifteen, checked myself into a boarding school on a scholarship, and never went back."

*Wow. Even I didn't leave that early.*

"Why would you do that? Home too stifling and constricting?"

Her laugh was harsh. "Yeah, if you call my stepfather drinking until he was rolling drunk every night, constricting."

I lifted my hand to encourage her to continue.

"What do you want me to say, David? My childhood, like so many before me, sucked. I never knew my father, my mother was always going out, doing her own thing, and her second husband was an asshole. I've been on my own a long time, and I know how to look after myself. I don't need her."

*But how well have you looked after yourself? And what would you do to acquire a husband that would mean you never had to work again?*

"So, you don't think you're like your mother?"

Jenika continued to walk around the large trees, running her hand along the bark. "Not at all. Are you like your father?"

That question stumped me for a moment. I opened my mouth to answer with a resounding *no*, but I had to re-think.

"A little maybe. We both enjoy success and money."

She rolled her eyes again like a teenager. "Yeah, but who doesn't? That doesn't make you the same as him, although, since meeting him, he seems like a nice man. But I know appearances can be deceiving."

I could hear the question in her answer and sighed.

"Let's sit."

There was an old park bench up ahead with a table and I took one side, while Jenika sat rigidly on the other.

"My father was rather devastated by my mother's death, and subsequently filled his bed and the house with women he didn't love. He had no idea how to be a good father and I basically raised myself."

Her eyes glinted with moisture and I looked away.

Eventually she said, "It sounds like we had a very similar life up to a point."

*Except that I have all the money in the world, and you don't. And I think that is always going to be a problem.*

"Maybe. But as a scientist I believe in the supremacy of genetics…" I turned around and faced her. "And your genes are going to determine who you are. Even if you don't like who your mother is, you will turn out like her."

I was told once that if you want to know what you'll get in the daughter, look to the mother and that will be your life in twenty-five years time.

I didn't like that prediction for my future.

I pushed myself to my feet and stared down at the woman who was now my stepsister.

*For better or worse.*

Her brown eyes were definitely shining with tears now.

"You're never going to forgive me for my mother, are you? Even though we're nothing alike. I don't give a damn about money, and she does. She's had a hundred lovers, and I've had two. I've spent my life proving to myself that I'm nothing like her, but you won't believe me, will you?"

Her words were touching but I had to be honest.

"Jenika, there's no point beating around the proverbial bush, okay? I'm sorry, but there is no way you can convince me that you aren't like your mother. For all I know, you both set us up to see who could marry first."

Her mouth gaped open. "I can show you years worth of phone records that show that I *never* even call my mother."

I shrugged. Could be fabricated, she could own a spare phone. I had no idea, and I didn't care. Cold encased my heart, and I felt the tug of pain when I looked at her now, and I didn't want that for my life.

Jenika pushed herself to her feet and I could see the tension in her muscles. Anger at being thwarted perhaps?

"David. I have spent months showing you who I am, because I know what I am. I am a good person, a generous woman. With my time, money and love. If you don't want me, you just have to say it. Don't give me some speech about how I'm going to turn out to be like my mother, who your father loves by the way. Because that's just punching below the belt."

I lifted my chin and hardened myself to the words that needed to be said. Despite the nagging thoughts calling at me to not commit myself too much to this rhetoric.

"Jenika, I don't want you. Last night was a mistake, and I think we should focus on trying to be the best step siblings possible."

Her head fell and I ignored the tears that dropped onto the dirt at her feet.

"I'm going to go back to the house to go through the books again." I said, wanting to get away from her.

She turned away so I couldn't see her face.

"That's fine. I'll be up later. Will we be leaving tonight?"

"Yes, I think that's best. I'll drop you home and put in a report to my father."

She nodded her head, but didn't say anymore.

I turned towards the huge house my father wanted to buy for his money-grubbing wife and couldn't shake the sadness swamping me.

The only way I was going to get over this one, was to replace Jenika as quickly as possible. And I knew just the woman.

I strode up the stairs and into the house. The mustiness was less heavy now and the wooden stair case glistened.

Yes. Jenika's mother would get my father, but they would not get me. I wanted a woman who loved me, not my money… and if I never found her, then at least I'd never have a child and repeat all the same mistakes my father had.

I went into the study and sat down to the books. All going ahead smoothly, I'd soon be able to go to my family home anytime I liked.

Because instead of the old brownstone being my father's property, it would be mine.

**6**

———

*J*ENIKA.

A week after we left my mother's new house, I woke up to find my period still hadn't arrived. It was due this week, I'm sure... But with all the stress, what's the bet I'm out of whack?

I pull out my phone and check my dates.

Unfortunately, I'm right, and my little calendar prompt says I should have started bleeding on Monday. It's Saturday. Five days past my date.

And I'm *never* late.

I throw my phone to the side and stare up and the ceiling. Oh God, what if I *am* pregnant?

*David will kill me!*

No, I can't possibly be.

My alarm goes off again and I groan. Why didn't I forget to turn my work alarm off today? I check the notification on my phone screen and close my eyes.

That's right. Because we have a new family 'event' on today, and I have to drive two hours to see my darling new stepbrother and his dad.

I roll out of bed and a wave of nausea hit me like a truck. My head spun and I closed my eyes forcing myself to take some deep, steadying breaths.

*What is that?*

I put my hand over the pain in my stomach and try to think why I'd feel this way.

Had I eaten dinner last night? No…I hadn't. Which was odd for me, but again, I was in mourning. Losing my relationship with David was hitting me harder than I thought it would. We'd only been together a few months, but I'd truly believed he was the man for me.

How could I have been so horribly wrong?

I'd trusted him. Given him everything I had, and he'd thrown it all back in my face. Believing, of all things, that I was with him for his money! Seriously?!

I opened my eyes and saw that the world around me had levelled out a bit.

*Good. Now stand up.*

I made my way to the sink and went to the toilet, still no blood, but my head was spinning. Probably lack of food more than anything.

I got dressed, did my hair in an elaborate braid that David had always liked, and grabbed some fruit. My stomach turned at the idea of anything else.

The car drive was long, and my head spun the whole time I was driving.

*Should I tell him that I might be pregnant?*

*No. He'll kill me. We've just agreed to keep the peace and try to be a family, and now he'll think I did this on purpose too.*

*Yeah, but the longer I wait, the more he'll think I've kept it from him.*

*Grrrr.*

I fought with myself for most of my drive and in the end, I decided that I wouldn't do a pregnancy test for a couple of days. After all, I could just be late due to stress, although I doubted it very much.

A baby. God, would that muck up everything! I didn't have the money to look after a baby, and I only had a few weeks vacation leave up my sleeve at work.

I shook my head and tried not to focus on the churning in my gut. My options were not good.

I arrived at the house and despite my tight belly and reservations, a peace descended on me that was like coming home.

David had told his father that we both loved the house and within a day it was bought, settled and my mother was packing up her stuff to move into her new home.

They'd asked us to come down for a family day house warming and of course I'd agreed.

I got out of the car and breathed in the fresh, peach-tainted air. I couldn't see David's car anywhere, so perhaps the workaholic hadn't taken the day off work?

A sigh of relief filtered through my body and I let my shoulders relax. That would be amazing. Not to have to see him today while I felt so unbalanced.

I grabbed my overnight bag and walked up the steps. The door opened before I even knocked.

"Jenny!" My mother beamed as she rushed forward to embrace me.

I didn't respond to start with. My mother rarely hugged me. But the longer she held me, the more I melted, until I hugged her back.

"Nice to see you, Mum."

"Please come in. You have to see everything!"

"I kind of already have.." I gently reminded her, but as I stepped into the house, I was blown away with how different it looked already.

"I've pulled all the curtains down and had all the windows cleaned. Got rid of all the knick knacks and put some of our own personal touches. What do you think?"

She'd removed some of the furniture and rearranged what was left so it was much less cluttered. I looked around the transformed living area and kept moving until we reached the kitchen. The house, which was once beautiful, was now alive.

"I love it, Mum. You've done an amazing job."

"Hasn't she?" her new husband repeated as he stepped into the kitchen with a huge smile on his face.

"Oh, it's only the start. I still want to do a lot more." My mother beamed.

"I know." He pulled my mum closer and kissed the top of her head.

Love filtered through me and I got that warm and fuzzy feeling that had always been missing from my interactions with my mother.

"You two look so happy." I couldn't help but say.

They laughed and Mum offered me a drink.

"Just water would be great." My stomach still wasn't great.

I couldn't help but ask. "No David today?"

"He's coming up later. Couldn't make it for lunch, but I think he'll be here by dinnertime."

"Oh, great." *Not!*

I relaxed into the kitchen chair and accepted my glass of water.

"Then I'd love to spend the day seeing more of your new home. I don't feel like I saw enough of it last time."

*I spent most of the day crying as I walked through the orchards last Saturday.*

"Absolutely." My stepfather answered.

Mum put a plate of biscuits in front of me, and they looked home baked.

"Don't tell me you cooked, Mum." I joked. Impossible.

She giggled. "Hardly. The local town has a bakery that is to die for. Isn't it, Jack?"

"Hmmm…" He agreed as he stuffed a jam-filled biscuit into his mouth.

I couldn't help but laugh. If this was any indication of how easily pleased this man was, then he and my mother would get along just fine.

"All right, what else do you want to show me?"


THE AFTERNOON PASSED QUICKLY and I helped Mum arrange two cupboards and the room that was now 'mine.'

Mum and Jack had of course taken the master suite with the four poster bed and I smiled every time I thought about it.

It was so naughty. Imagine what they'd say if they knew David and I had sex on that bed?

The sun set and dinner was ready. Mum had always been an alright sort of cook, as long as you stuck to meat and vegetables and as the smell of roasted lamb met my nostrils, I sighed with relief.

*No failed attempt at lasagne or curry tonight.*

I walked into the living room where Jack had lit the fire and sat on one of the newly cleaned, comfortable couches.

"Oh, here he is. This must be the new girlfriend he's been telling me about," Jack said as he walked to the front door to greet his son.

*Whaaattttt?*

My heart stuttered to a halt as David stepped into the entrance, and then walked into the lounge room with a tall blonde in a red dress, a high slit revealing a shapely thigh.

*Oh fuck. No.*

"Hey Dad. Everyone. This is Tania. Tania, this is my father, Jack., my new stepmother, Sue, and her daughter, Jenika."

David eyes met mine for a brief moment before flitting away to settle on his new girlfriend.

My stomach retched and I gagged. Oh no. I put my hand over my mouth and bolted out of the room. Straight to the bathroom.

I spewed into my hand as I ran but I kept moving, gagging over and over until I got into the small cubicle and managed to get my head over the bowl, throwing the contents of my hand in along with it.

Sweat formed on my brow and my eyes squeezed shut.

*What the hell is he doing? Tormenting me like this. That just isn't fair David... not fair.*

I wiped my mouth with a towel and slid to the floor next to the toilet.

*How could he be so cruel?*

~

*DAVID*

*Whoa. That was an even more dramatic reaction than I'd expected.*

Sure, I'd thought Jenika might throw wine at me, or slap my face. Two reactions that would have indicated our past, but I was ready for anything. Especially since I'd moved on. Sort of.

But to go pale and run out of the room vomiting was a whole other level.

"What was that about?" Dad asked.

"I don't know. I better go check she's okay," Sue said and hurried after her.

Tania gave me a knowing look and I ignored her. Tania was an old flame who I'd rung the moment my Dad had asked me to come down for a housewarming dinner.

I'd barely slept all week, knowing the only woman that I'd ever truly connected with was now out of bounds forever. But Tania was happy to fill the void, though for me, even the thought of kissing her didn't do anything for me.

"Tania, it's so lovely to meet you."

Dad took her away to the couch and offered her a drink.

She'd drink all night and barely touch dinner, which would be an absolute pain in the ass. But what else could you do if you wanted a size zero ass?

Sue stepped back into the room, her smile now a ghost of the one she usually gave me.

"Jenika's not well. I'm not sure she'll be up for dinner."

"What's wrong?" Dad asked her and I pulled Tania close to me. One always needed a shield if the world was about to go to hell.

"I think it's my fault," Sue confided. "She helped me today we spent the whole day cleaning, and I knew she wasn't feeling well as it was. She's barely eaten all day and now she's vomiting. Maybe she has a stomach flu?"

Tania grimaced and glanced up at me. "I can't afford to get sick. I have a commercial shoot on Monday."

*Perfect excuse to get out of here.*

"Well, we'll stay for dinner and then head back. We don't need to stay overnight."

That at least would stop me from having to make up lame excuses for why I didn't want to fuck her in my dad's house, around the corner from my ex-girlfriend.

Luckily Tania couldn't hear my thoughts, because she gave me a seductive smile that indicated she was happy with that idea, and I let Sue and Dad hustle us into the dining room.

"I really like your new house. It's pretty," Tania gushed as she folded herself into one of the chairs.

"Thank you, dear." Sue said, her gaze meeting mine with the acuity of a woman who knew how to assess people better than most.

I lifted one eyebrow and stared back.

*Yeah, I know she's dumb. Not the reason I'm with her.*

She did a strange eye roll and I found myself wanting to laugh. That was where Jenika got it from.

"I'll go get dinner," Sue said with a smile and headed off to the kitchen.

She came back not long later, serving lamb roast and vegetables and followed by a beautiful pie for dessert.

With my belly full, I complimented the chef. "That was really good, Sue. I didn't realise you could cook."

She laughed. "You don't know me, David, and that is totally fine. I can't bake to save my life, but I can do a decent roast."

I nodded and wiped my mouth with a napkin. I checked my watch and calculated that we needed to stay another hour or so, and then I could get out of here.

"Are you enjoying the house? Happy to get out of the city?"

Dad nodded and Sue smiled. "Absolutely. I love the house so much and really can't believe this is where I live. Every time I leave and come home I think, wow... I live here."

My gaze swung to my dad's and his eyes shadowed.

Jenika stood at the door. "Mum, please don't talk like that. David already thinks you're a gold digger and you're just accentuating the point."

Her voice was like a shot gun in the room and silence fell like a lead balloon.

Jenika's face was ashen white and the pain of my guilt hit me in the gut like a sucker punch.

"Jenika…" I said, the need to apologise overwhelming me.

"Jenny! Don't say things like that. Surely David knows I love his father." Sue's shrill voice rang through the air and Jenika continued to glare at me.

"Hardly, Mum. Anyway, I just wanted to say goodnight." She turned away.

"We're leaving after dinner," I explained, hoping to alleviate her stress.

"Good."

"Jenny! What is wrong with you tonight?" Sue asked, getting to her feet and walking over to where her daughter stood trembling.

Jenika dragged her gaze away from me and concentrated on Sue who was now in front of her.

"I didn't tell you, Mum… I was dating this pretty amazing guy for a few months and he dumped me last weekend. For no reason. At all. And I am…" Her voice trembled and I could see the tears in her eyes.

She backed away, shaking her hands. "I'm sorry, Mum. I'm sorry Jack. I need to go."

She turned and fled and my throat tightened as though she'd wrapped her hands around my neck.

Sue wandered back to the table and fell down in her chair with a confused shake of her head.

"Whoa… what a psycho." Tania giggled from beside me and my heart clunked with the mistake I'd made.

"Ah. I think we need to go. I'm so sorry your housewarming isn't what it should be, Sue. Dad."

I pushed myself to my feet and grabbed my 'date,' for the night.

"Let's go."

Dad and Sue walked us to the door and not for the first time did I notice the easy affection between them.

"Thank you for coming, I hope you have a safe trip home," Sue said as Dad's hand slipped naturally around her waist.

I believed she actually meant it despite the look of concern on her face.

"Thanks."

She opened her mouth and then shut it again. I knew she wanted to ask me about what Jenika said but I wasn't in the mood to deal with her. My emotions were too raw, too hurt.

I shook Dad's hand and took my date to the car. She pressed close and I wanted to toss her away, which unfortunately I couldn't do.

"Let's go."

"Yes." She slid into the car and purred like a kitten.

I threw my sports car into gear and hit the accelerator. I needed to get back into the city and back to my old life.

I'd been so unfocused this week and I had a slew of interviews and work travel ahead of me in preparation for the new football shoe launch.

It was time to get my head back into the game, and stop worrying about a girl named Jenika.

7

———

*J*ENIKA.

The weeks went by and I couldn't put the pregnancy tests or the doctor's appointments off another moment.

I went to my local doc and got the official diagnosis that I was nine weeks pregnant. Not that I needed to be told. After a month of morning, afternoon, and evening sickness, sore boobs and no period, I'd been pretty sure I knew what was going on.

Unfortunately, I also knew how it had happened. I wasn't on the pill because it made me feel terrible and we had used condoms most of the time. But David had used withdrawal when we'd been in the shower, and in the limo once or twice.

*Damn this is my fault.*

I shook my head and took a deep breath to stave off the swell of misery coming at me. I wanted nothing more than to curl into a ball and stay in bed for a month, but like the responsible adult I was trying to be, I went to class, determined to focus only on the future.

I had rights to child support from David, but that would mean handing over custody too, and I wasn't sure I wanted that for my child. It would mean that my baby would be exposed to all the women he was dating. Brainless twits would be in and out of my child's life, and I couldn't think of anything worse for him or her.

After a lifetime of bad parental relationships, for both me and David, I was determined to break the cycle and love my child above all else.

Yes. That was the strategy.

I would deal with David's rights, and money issues later, but for now I needed to just focus on putting one foot in front of the other.

Three more weeks went by and I saw David's picture splashed all over the newspapers and online media. His new shoes were a major success and the football association wanted to award him for another brilliant design.

If I was looking for a smart daddy for my baby, I couldn't have picked a better one really.

I rubbed my still flat belly and sighed. Thirteen weeks, almost. I couldn't believe it.

I gathered my work things and headed out to the car. Another weekend down at Mum's house. I'd been going there at the end of each week lately and I'd come to realise that I enjoyed having her in my life.

We were different, sure. But she'd changed a lot in the eight years since I'd left home and I enjoyed our time together now.

When I arrived, nauseous and tired, I was shocked to see David's car parked on the driveway.

*What are you doing here?*

I grabbed my bags and walked up to the front door. Hopefully he was only dropping in for another flying visit, because the last time I'd seen him a month ago, he hadn't been able to wait to race that leggy blonde home to his bed.

My stomach turned as I pushed open the door, the sound of soft music and glasses clinking getting my attention.

"What are we celebrating?" I asked, forcing the words past my tight throat.

David stood by the fire, holding a large glass of red wine and wearing a tight grey shirt that accentuated his gorgeous shape.

"David just signed a massive contract with the biggest soccer star in the world." My mother squealed and I grimaced.

"Wonderful. Congratulations, David."

My gaze wandered around the room. Where was the model thing? "No girlfriend tonight?"

He simply shook his head, which didn't really answer my question. Was he still with her or had he moved on to someone equally as hideous?

"Mum, I'll just put my bag in my room and lie down if that's okay? I'm not feeling very well."

"Oh, Jenny. Come have one drink with us before you retire."

I glanced at the stairs that beckoned me. To the shower that would ease my tight and sore low back. But then I looked back at the family by the fire. To Mum's eager smile and the man whose embrace I missed as much as a desert ached for rain.

It was a moment of great weakness and I succumbed.

"All right."

I dropped my bag at the foot of the stairs and walked over to the group.

"Wine, Jenny?" Mum asked and I shook my head.

*Not a chance.*

"No thanks. I'm asleep on my feet as it is. Water please, Mum."

She tottered off to the kitchen and David's gaze met mine. I was expecting the disdain I'd seen so often since our parents wedding, but instead there was concern, and a heat that made tears gather in my eyes.

"Are you okay?" he asked and the pain in my back twinged, hard.

"Ah…. Yeah… I think."

I put my hand to my back and gasped as a wave of nausea passed through me.

I needed to distract myself, and fast. I could feel the walls that I'd built up over the past few weeks tumbling down around me.

I really had no defences when it came to this man. I grabbed for my mother's glass and held it up. Blinking against the tears buffeting my system.

"To you. May you accumulate more and more accolades and wealth, David. It seems to be the only important thing in your life and I'm glad you have bucket loads of it."

His gaze hardened and I knew I'd gone too far with that one. But I didn't care. If I felt like shit, then so could he.

"I don't think he feels that way, Jenika." Jack quietly corrected me and pain hit me head on.

The wine glass fell from my hand and red liquid splashed all over the cream carpet like a grotesque murder scene.

"Jenika!" My mother said as she ran back into the room, a loud cry making her displeasure known for the mess.

I collapsed in on myself, staggering to the couch as the cramps got stronger and my panic took over.

"Oh no. Oh no. Please, no. Not now."

I couldn't lose the baby, not here, not now.

*Please hold on, no matter what I've said, I want you. I really do. Please don't leave me.*

"What is it? What's wrong?"

It was David's insistent voice, his hands surrounding me, holding me up where I would have fallen to the floor.

I gulped for air, trying to calm myself.

I ran a hand inside my skirt, feeling for the wetness I was sure would be there between my legs.

I dragged my hand back out, a spot of blood on my fingertips. Horror gripped my heart like the hand of death.

"No…"

I raised my gaze to David's, the worry on his face at odds with the feelings he'd professed to have for me.

"What's wrong?"

I gulped, swallowing the tears the rose, though some leaked down my face. I needed to get help, now.

"I'm losing the baby."

David's eyes opened so wide it was suddenly like he was part of a cartoon.

Mum grabbed at me and pulled me to her. "Baby? You're pregnant? To who?"

*I was pregnant. That would soon be in the past.*

"Mum, please. Just take me to the hospital. I need to get to the hospital."

The pain was lessening now, but I could feel more blood. It would be a miracle if my baby survived the night.

"I'll take her." David's strong voice broke through the fog of clatter around me and he wrapped me in a blanket from the couch.

"You don't need to do that, son. We'll help her..." Jack's soft voice sounded worried for me.

"No." David snapped at them, putting a strong arm beneath my legs and lifting me up into his embrace.

I let the sobs overwhelm me and clung to my lover. My stepbrother. My love.

He started running and I closed my eyes and let the nightmare engulf me.

**8**

_______

*D*AVID.

"How is she?" I asked the doctor who had squirted cold lube on Jenika's belly and was moving a metal thing around her pubic area.

The doctor didn't answer and I stared at Jenika where she lay in the hospital bed. Tears streamed down her face and she was as pale as the sheets.

*Why hadn't she told me? Maybe it wasn't mine?*

My own subconscious scoffed at me there. *Who else's would it be?*

"Ah, there it is. You are one lucky lady."

"What? What do you mean?" Jenika asked, her head shooting up and her eyes fixing on the little black and white screen.

"There it is. Heart beat's good, measuring… twelve weeks and three days. The bleeding could be a sign that a miscarriage is eminent but at the moment, the baby's still alive and well. We'll keep you in for a few days to monitor you, just in case."

"Why is she bleeding?" I asked. "That can't be normal."

"Well, for some women it is. Some bleed for a lot of their pregnancy, especially if there is a lot of stress. Other times, it is an indication of miscarriage, so we'll take it one day at a time."

My gut clenched and twisted. With worry and fear, which was surprising. This wasn't a baby I wanted, nor even knew about up until an hour ago. And now, the last thing I wanted to hear, was that it might be gone too soon.

Jenika sat up and reached for the tissue box, wiping her face and blowing her nose. "Thank you, Doctor."

"Get some rest," he said patting her arm politely, and then shutting the door behind him as he left.

I took a long breath in and out, then stood up. Not sure how I should even start this conversation.

Jenika started it instead. "Yes, it's yours. No, I didn't tell you. Would I have, maybe at some stage, but I hadn't figured out what I was going to do yet."

I fell back into my chair.

"Why?"

"Why what?"

"Why didn't you tell me as soon as you knew?"

I kinda knew the answer to this, but I still needed her to say it. I'd already calculated it in my head, and she would have worked out she was pregnant very soon after we broke up. Or, I'd refused to see her for more than what her mother was.

She shrugged and picked up the edge of the horrible hospital gown she wore.

"I realised it could be a possibility around the time we came up to the new house. But I didn't know for sure, and I was still trying to sort things out with you. Then you made it clear that you wanted nothing to do with me." She gave a big sigh and my chest tightened. "I avoided going to the doctor that week and thought we'd talk about it after our parents' dinner thing, but then your brought Tania, and you know how that went."

"You knew then?" *All that time and you kept it from me?*

She glared at me. "No, I did not! But my period was late so I knew it was possible. Anyway, you turned up with your girlfriend and made it perfectly clear you didn't want me in your life, so done really."

"You didn't think I had a right to know? As the father." I tried not to raise my voice. She still looked incredibly fragile and had been through enough of a trauma tonight.

*But, still...Fuck!*

"What, so you could accuse me of trying to get pregnant on purpose? For trying to trap you and take all your money? Yeah, like I was going to walk into that fire storm for no reason." Jenika shot straight back.

"I wouldn't have done that," I said.

*You probably would have you know...*

I would have been furious, sure. That she'd achieved something that so many had tried before her. They'd failed, and she'd succeeded, although I wasn't sure how.

"How did this even happen? We were so careful." Except for the once or twice I'd forgotten condoms and pulled out, but it couldn't have been that, could it?

*The shower wasn't exactly a successful withdrawal. Remember the feeling of pulsing inside her?*

She shrugged again, nestled down into the bed and turned her head away from me.

Had she done this on purpose? And if she did, why hadn't she told me earlier?

"Thank you for bringing me in, David, but you can go back to your girlfriend now. Ask my mum to come in tomorrow, okay?"

I was being dismissed and I didn't like it.

"Jenika."

"I am not your concern any more, I never really was. Please go. More than likely that little blip on the screen will be gone by morning, and you can stop pretending you care."

"I do care about you, Jenika."

I always had. Since the first moment I saw her smile, I hadn't stopped caring. Maybe it was time to tell her the truth. To admit that Tania was nothing more than a red herring for my father and the world.

"Tania is..."

Jenika rolled onto her side and faced the wall, drawing the white sheet up to her shoulder.

"Good night, David."

Obviously now wasn't the time for that conversation. But it was time to face up to my mistakes and my responsibilities.

I stood up and pulled the blanket up over Jenika's body, the tears on her cheeks a testament to the pain she was still in.

"Do you want me to call the doctor again?"

"No."

"Alright. Well, I'm only a phone call away if you need me."

She didn't answer but I was pretty sure she would have said, 'I don't need you.'

Because I was pretty sure she didn't. She would have continued on whatever path she was on without me and I might never have known the child she had conceived.

I got out of the small hospital room, shut the door and went in search of the doctor.

I had to wait half an hour in the waiting room, but eventually he found me, now in hospital scrubs.

"You wanted to speak to me?" he asked, obviously annoyed that I had disturbed him.

Well, that was just tough.

"Yes. I want to know what the likelihood is of Jenika losing the baby?"

His mouth twisted to the side. "There is no answer to that."

And there probably wasn't. The universe worked in mysterious ways. But there had to be some statistics he could quote for me.

"I know, and I won't hold you on it. I just want to know how to prepare myself."

He blew out a breath and put a hand on one hip. "Well, look. The likelihood of her miscarrying, considering the amount of blood she's lost, is higher than her chances of carrying this pregnancy to term."

My heart fell, as must my face, because the doctor gave me a lopsided smile. "The fact that the foetus is still alive, the heartbeat strong…they're all good signs. Don't lose all hope, but we have no way of changing the natural outcome of this. What the body chooses to do, is what will be."

"And you think the stress…. might have caused it."

*If this was my fault I will never forgive myself.*

"Stress can cause miscarriage, yes. But at the same time, I've seen women beaten up, living in war torn countries and half-starved, get through a whole pregnancy and deliver a healthy baby. There's never a rhyme nor reason for this."

That gave me some comfort but at the same time, part of me knew that if I hadn't broken up with Jenika when I had, this may not have happened.

How much did I really care about my money? Was Jenika right, and that was all I now amounted to?

"Thank you, Doctor."

I left and drove around for a while. I considered going straight back to the city, but part of me knew I needed to stand up and tell our parents the truth. If she kept the baby, then it would all come out anyway.

So, sometime after midnight, I went home to their house. Everyone was asleep and I wasn't going to wake them to explain what was going on.

I got a few hours sleep before my insomnia kicked in and I heard the clock chime three.

*Time to work.*

I got up and was sitting at my computer in the study as the sun rose over the orchard.

"How long have you been awake?" my father asked, rubbing his eyes.

*Too long, but I've got heaps of work done.* "Oh, a few hours. You?"

"Five minutes. I wanted to know… how's Jenika?" My father's worried face kicked me in the gut. He'd come to care for her, and I didn't blame him. She was a good woman.

"I'm not sure how she is this morning, I haven't spoken to her yet."

But I would remedy that as soon as I could. Eight am would be alright to visit her, I was sure.

"I mean, last night. Did you find out what's happened to her?"

I nodded. "Yes. She was still pregnant as of last night. But the doctor said she'll probably miscarry if the bleeding keeps going. He said there's no stopping the body's natural… whatever."

Dad took a seat in the chair opposite me, his face filled with concern. "Oh, poor girl. Did she tell you who the father is? I didn't realise she was seeing anyone," Dad asked.

"How well do you know her, Dad?"

He sighed. "Well enough, or so I thought. She's been coming up here every weekend since we moved in, spending time with Sue and I. Healing their rift, or whatever Sue said. They had a falling out a few years ago, I think, and Sue desperately wants their relationship to be better."

"Do you think Jenika is like her mother?" I asked, well knowing the answer I would get would be stacked. My father seemed to actually care for his new wife.

"In some ways… I suppose. But Jenika seems much more down to earth, honest. She's a nice girl…." My father's gaze narrowed and he stared at me. "Why David? How well do you know Jenika?"

"Better than you." I said, though I couldn't smile at my lame joke.

I took a deep breath and faced up to my responsibilities. "The baby's mine."

"What?" Sue's voice came from the doorway and we both turned to see her standing in the hall gaping at me. "That baby's *yours*? How is that possible?"

"Come sit down, Sue." Dad tapped the chair next to him and she shuffled into the room and sat down, her back ramrod straight and her lips thinned in displeasure.

"Go," she demanded.

Dad put a comforting arm around her but she didn't relax into him as she normally would.

"How is my daughter?"

"She's still pregnant, or was when I was with her last night."

"And why did you abandon her?"

"I didn't abandon her, Sue."

She gave me an evil eye. "Then how come you didn't know she was pregnant? And how was it that you were even sleeping with my daughter? And how could you bring that stupid girlfriend of yours to our home?"

Her voice got harsher and harsher as she spoke and I found myself cringing like a young boy in the principal's office.

Honesty was probably the best way to go in this situation.

"Jenika and I were dating for two months before your wedding. We didn't realise you guys even knew each other."

My dad chuckled. "No wonder you were both so strange at the wedding."

"Yes. We were shocked, and I was pretty angry. I believed she'd done it on purpose, or something…. and I ended it."

Sue snorted at me. "Why would you do that? Just because we joked about you two being family now, doesn't mean you actually are. You're not blood relatives and you didn't grow up together. It's not like it would be incest or anything."

Worry tugged at me heart as I watched Sue step in to bat for her daughter. Money was everything to this woman, and I knew she'd love to have her daughter married off well.

I clenched my teeth and spat out the truth. "I didn't trust Jenika after meeting you. I know you're only with my father for his money and the last thing I wanted was a marriage like that."

The shocked gasp that came from my stepmother was expected, so I let my gaze wander to my father.

His eyes were hard. "How dare you say that? How could you do that to the girl?"

I shrugged, unable to answer the question. Looking back now it was hard to see where my logic lay.

Dad continued. "Did you have any indication that she was interested in your money?"

I thought back with a clear mind and shook my head. "No. If anything, she preferred to do low key things that required no money. She never let me buy her anything other than dinner."

"Yes! How could you do that to poor Jenika?" Sue spat at me, jumping to her feet. "I will ignore your accusations that I only married your father for his money, because he obviously hasn't told you what lengths he went to, to put a prenuptial agreement in place. Instead I'm going to tell you that you are a horrible judge of character, and the lowest of the low. My daughter is the kindest, sweetest girl I know. And to answer that smirk, she is nothing like me. She's barely even had a boyfriend, and you think she'd be trying to trap you for money? You're sick. And I want you out of this house. Now."

I looked towards my father and he stood up, putting an arm around his wife.

"Go, son. We'll look after Jenika."

I stood up, feeling as small as a mouse.

"No. She's my responsibility." I couldn't leave.

Sue glared up at me. "No, she's not. She's mine. And I have failed that girl enough in her lifetime, I won't do it again. Leave David. Now." She was looking at me with all the anger and hatred of a mother lion and for the first time I found myself warming to my new stepmother.

"Call me when you find out how she is. Please."

Sue crossed her arms over her chest and Dad gave me the slightest nod. So, I went. Back to my car, back to my apartment, back to the city that I treasured.

Without the woman I loved.

# 9

*J*ENIKA.

"Are you sure you should go home already? If you can stay in the hospital a bit longer it's probably best, Jenny."

I cringed at the drone of my mother's voice, God love her. Because I was sick of her already.

"Mum. I'm fine. I want to go home. Get back to work. Get on with my life." That was the best way to be, and always had been. Just keep moving forward.

Mum huffed, and reached to grip my hand. "But you're still pregnant."

And I was. Thank God, or whoever was looking over me.

The bleeding and cramps had stopped, the baby was still firmly fastened, and the morning sickness was still kicking my ass.

*Definitely pregnant.*

"I know. And I'll be careful. But I can't afford to take any more time off work." I had to save up my leave for when I really needed it.

Mum waved her hand in a dismissive way. "Oh, Jenny don't worry about that. Jack said he'll help you with all your expenses. After all, this is his grandchild as well."

*I didn't want to rely on anyone's help, but it was lovely of him to offer.*

"I know, Mum. Thank you, but I'll be alright." Jack had offered me whatever financial assistance I wanted when he'd come to visit yesterday. I'd been shocked to find out that David had owned up to everything, but Jack had been lovely really. "You picked well there, mum. He's really, a nice man."

"Yes. He is," Mum said with a smile. Third time really was the charm for her.

We got in the car and drove back to Mum and Jack's house. "I need to drive home tonight, Mum. Where's my car? I was hoping I could go home tonight."

It was Monday, and the second last week of school.

"Jack put it in the garage. He's asked someone he knows to drive you home tomorrow some time. Don't worry, I called your work and told them you were ill."

I groaned. "Of course, you did. Well, what am I meant to do until then?"

The last thing I wanted was to be stuck on a couch with nothing to do, while my mum made annoying comments about her sports wizard impending grandchild.

My talents weren't enough, no. But, she was rapt with the father's genetics however.

"Just rest. That's what the doctors said to do, didn't they?"

I groaned and dragged myself out of the car Jack had bought for her. Some sort of luxury SUV and it was nice, but just reminded me of the gold digging aspect of her personality that David had accused me of having too.

"Come in and have a cup of tea."

"A cup of tea? You know I don't drink tea, Mother."

I trudged up the stairs, not wanting anything but a warm bath and a bed to crawl into.

"I hope your stepson has gone home and hopefully moved on with his life with that horrible girlfriend of his." I threw over my shoulder.

"Oh, he has. But he doesn't have the girlfriend anymore, hasn't for weeks."

*Huh? Since when?*

I swivelled around at the top of the stairs and stared at my mother. "What? How do you know?"

"Jack told me about it yesterday. He gave David quite the grilling and got all the details out of him. It seems that they weren't really together at all. Some old bed partner he paid to come here and pretend she was his girlfriend. The nerve of him really." Mum shook her head in disgust.

My brain wasn't working fast enough to keep up with her. Which, I imagined, was the first time since I was six-years-old and realised I was smarter than my mother.

"I don't get it, Mum."

"Come sit on the couch, sweetheart. You don't need to retreat to your bedroom just yet." She reached out a hand to me and I couldn't stop myself from walking back down the stairs and allowing her to tug me into the living room and pushing me down into the comfortable couch.

"I'll go get you a hot chocolate. Be back soon."

Mum disappeared into the kitchen and David appeared around the couch like an apparition, his normally suited up body clad only in jeans and a white T-shirt that made me stare.

He was so unbelievably gorgeous it hurt to look at him.

So, I didn't. I turned my face away.

He moved closer, sitting on the couch next to me and taking my hands in his. I curled my legs up under me.

"What are you doing, David?" I tried to pull my hands away again, but he held tight.

"I need to talk to you."

Tears gathered in my eyes, hot and stinging. "No. Please. I can't handle anymore."

"Why? Has something happened to the baby?"

The way he said *baby* made my stomach flip and I tried not to let my hopes rise from the floor where they'd been smashed for weeks.

"No. I'm still pregnant for the moment, but I don't want to talk about it, because I'll cry again and I'm beyond dehydrated."

He let go of my hands only to lift his arm up and cup my face.

"I am so sorry for the way I've treated you, Jenika."

I lifted my head away from his touch and looked at him again. He actually sounded genuine.

"Oh, really? What are you sorry for David?"

*For breaking up with me for, no fault of my own? For abandoning me when I needed you? For comparing me to my mother!*

"For everything. But mostly for not giving you a chance to explain. I didn't trust that you were the person I'd believed you were. I was an idiot."

"You were. I'm sorry, David, but there is no way you can undo what's been done. And if this is all for the sake of the baby, you needn't worry. This is officially a high risk pregnancy, so please don't expect anything from me. I could miscarry at any moment."

I waited for him to jump away or sneer in disgust, but instead he looked sad.

"I'm so sorry you don't trust me anymore. I earned that trust and then destroyed it."

"Yes, you did. After getting through all my relationship issues and trusting that you would be different, you were just as bad as the boys at school who used to grope me in the hallways, assuming I was as easy as my mother."

"I'm sorry."

I pushed my legs to the floor and sat up straighter.

"Stop saying you're sorry. We had barely got to know each other before you tossed me out the door, so stop acting like we had this long future ahead of us. We didn't."

I got to my feet, my breathing labored. He couldn't fix this, I wouldn't let him. I couldn't be with a man who was trapped into being with me. That would be the worst thing in the world.

"I know you think this baby gives you no choice, but that's just not how I feel. Just pretend I got pregnant off some guy at a bar one night, and that you don't know me like you do. Then we can go back to our lives and you'll be free of all responsibilities."

He got to his feet as well. "I want to show you something."

He walked over to the coffee table and spun around his laptop. I waited as he tapped on the keys, my frustration growing by the second.

"David, I'm going to bed. Please don't be here when I wake up."

"No. Stop, please just look."

I rolled my eyes and stepped towards him.

"What am I looking at?"

"This is my diary. Date stamped and unalterable. I want you to see what I wrote the morning before our parents wedding."

I just stared at him for a full minute, not wanting to do what he asked, but knowing this was probably the only way to get away from him.

"Fine."

I dropped to the floor and knelt beside the ancient coffee table, focusing on the date before I lifted my gaze to read what he'd written.

It was mostly about work, then me. Our night together. Heat rose in my face as he recalled the way we made love and then the last line stopped my heart.

*She said she loved me and for the first time in my life, the words seemed right. This is a woman I can see myself marrying.*

I fell back and shuffled across the carpet until I could pull myself up into the armchair.

I just stared at open space for a moment, my heart thumping against my ribs as the revelation took time to sink in. The cream carpet grew fuzzy in front of my glazed eyes and heat stung my nose.

*What did this mean?*

I blinked several times and raised my gaze to meet David's.

He sat on the couch, leaning towards me.

"Why did you show me that?"

"Because I wanted to prove to you that I'm not trying to get back with you for the sake of the baby. I've always wanted you and I can't believe I let a stupid thing like our parents getting married affect that."

I wiped at the tears dripping down my face. What a joke.

"That wasn't the only reason. You thought I was a gold digger like my mother."

He shook his head sadly. "I was wrong. About both of you. My dad and I had a heart to heart talk, and your mother seems to share genuine affection with him."

"I know, which was a bit of a surprise for me too, to be honest."

"And you're nothing like that anyway, Jenika, I know that."

"How do you know that?"

He shrugged. "Deep down I always knew that. I've learnt to be a good judge of character, and your heart shines through like a beacon."

I looked at him pretty sure I had a sceptical look on my face. "Seriously? Now you're trusting your gut? Now that I'm pregnant?"

He cringed. "Yeah, well…I'd like to think that I would have got my shit together and come to my senses at some point, but this was a huge wake up call, yes."

I took a deep breath and relaxed my posture. "Look David, if this is about the baby, we can work all that out later. I'd never keep it from you, if that's what you want. You can have as much access as you want, and I don't need anything from you moneywise. Maybe some help with schooling later on but—"

He held up his hand to stop me.

"Please don't placate me. We'll deal with the possibility of a child later. I want to talk about us first."

*Huh? You said there was no 'us.'*

"Us?"

"Yes."

"All right." I crossed my arms and slid back in my chair. I didn't know how to process all of this. It was too much, all at once. "I'm glad you've come to the right conclusion about me. I never cared about your money, even less so now since you have such huge hang ups about it."

Rosy color lit up David's face and I was surprised to see it.

"Don't tell me that embarrassed you David, because honestly, it's pretty clear where your priorities lie. I loved you, trusted you. And you threw all of it back in my face at the first sign of trouble. I have no reason to believe you won't do it again."

He cleared his throat as though preparing a speech.

"Jenika. I want a second chance. Another chance to show you I can be a decent man, a good father. I may not have had the best example, but I'm sure I can work it out."

I could hear the pain behind the words and I couldn't help asking more.

"What do you mean?"

"I mean, my mum died before I even remember her and my father spent my life avoiding me and focusing on a parade of women not suitable to replace my mother."

I cringed. "Ouch. But, what does that have to do with anything?"

"I had no confidence in my ability to have a relationship that could stand the test of time, but with you, I want to try. And succeed. I'm sure you can teach me how to love you the way you need me to."

I choked on a laugh. "I only wanted you to trust me. Talk to me. Cuddle me the way you would at night. Everything was perfect and you stuffed it all up."

"And I'll make it up to you."

*I'm not sure that you can.*

"I know you don't need presents, but I got you this."

He handed me a small black box and my heart clenched as it beat faster. That looked suspiciously like a ring box.

"Is this what I think it is, David? Because if it is…"

*It couldn't be.*

"Open it and see."

My hands trembled as I tried to open the box. It wouldn't give initially, and then it sprung open like a jack in the box.

I stared. I gasped. My heart raced.

I couldn't believe it.

"But, why?" I asked, lifting my gaze from the perfect solitaire ring that sat on the velvet.

It had to be two carats, maybe three. I had no idea about jewellery, but it would weigh my finger down considerably.

"Because I want you in my life, and you deserve to have a sign from me of that."

He shifted closer and reached out for my hands. This time I let him take them.

"I've never given anyone else a piece of jewellery like this. Never asked a woman this question."

He slid to his knees and I gaped at him.

"Jenika. I want you to marry me. Today, tomorrow, in a year, in ten years. I don't care. That is for you to decide, but for now, I want you to wear this ring as a sign of the promise I'm making you. To love you, to be loyal to you, to give you anything in the world that you want, if you'll give me another chance at a life with you."

Fear gripped my heart not allowing the hope to spring forth that I knew was there.

"But what if I lose the baby, David?"

*I can't have that be the only reason you're with me.*

His face softened and his lips picked up at the sides in a smile. "Then we cry, and go on a holiday, and recover however you like. But I still want you. I want to go back to the time before the wedding, and move forward as we'd planned. More dinner, more days in bed…"

"Days?" I grinned at him. "You'd take a day off work?"

His face sobered. "I'd do anything for you Jenika. I'm so incredibly sorry."

I took a long, shuddering breath and looked back at the ring.

"You know this is too big, right?" I joked as I picked it up out of its nest.

"Doesn't it fit? I thought my guess might have been pretty good."

He took the engagement ring from me and slipped it on my fourth finger. On my left hand. And although snug, it was a perfect fit.

A strangled giggle burst through my lips.

"See." He said, sounding happy that he'd been right.

I whacked him softly with my hand, my gaze glued to the ring.

"It's still too big. I won't be able to fit through the door."

He laughed, "Yeah, part of me knew you'd want something more modest, but I didn't want you thinking I'd picked something cheap for you either. So, I got the one I liked, and if you want something different, we'll go buy you it tomorrow."

Another one? He had to be kidding.

"No. I love it. Thank you."

He touched my chin with his fingers and lifted my face up to his. Our eyes met and a warm sigh filled up my chest.

"So that's a yes? You'll marry me when you're ready?"

I smiled at his hopeful face. "I promise to give us the best go possible, and if that happens at some point, then that would be amazing too."

He whooped and pulled me into his lap, kissing my forehead and nose.

I lifted my lips to his and let my love for him rise to the surface.

"I love you, David."

"And I love you."

He pressed his lips to mine and I let the warmth and safety that he'd always represented swamp me.

I had no idea if we'd last past tomorrow, but he was giving us another chance at a life we'd both once foreseen, and that was all I needed.

# EPILOGUE

*One year later*

JENIKA.

Mum and Jack's estate looked amazing. The marquee next to the orchard was massive, and decked out in the most beautiful linens, silver and china.

Mum had gone nuts on the floral arrangements, the invitations, the guest list and the menu. The amount of money she'd spent was mind boggling .

The only real input I'd had into my own wedding, had been to pick the dress.

Which was kind of amazing, even if I did say so myself.

"Wow, Jenika. You look incredible." Jack said as he walked up to the mirror and looked at me.

I stared at myself for a moment, taking in the vision of the perfect bride I'd never really dreamt about before. After so many years of avoiding meaningful relationships, I was finally getting my happily ever after.

"Thanks, Jack."

I turned to smile at my stepfather who would soon become my

father-in-law as well.

"Shall we?"

"Yes, but before we do, I need to say something."

I waited as Jack cleared his throat and pulled himself together. "You have made my son happier than I ever thought possible. He's become the man I always hoped he'd be, and ten times the father I ever was. And I want you to know that you will have my undying love for that, forever."

Tears sprung to my eyes and I waved my hands at my face.

"Oh Jack, that's beautiful, but if you make me cry and ruin all my makeup run, Mum will kill you."

That broke the mood and Jack chortled.

"You're right, and we better get out there before she comes running in to hurry us up."

I pulled my small veil down over my face and check myself in the mirror once more.

"Alright. Let's go."

I grabbed my posy of pink and white roses, and tucked my hand into Jack's elbow.

We walked out of the main bedroom where I'd gotten ready and walked slowly down the stairs.

I was a good ten pounds too heavy still, since the birth of our daughter five months ago, but I was healthy. And David couldn't keep his hands off me.

"You nervous?" Jack whispered at me and I giggled.

"Hardly. I'm worried he'll have changed his mind by the time we get there."

Jack took another careful, slow step down the stairs.

"Hardly. My son would rather give up his company than lose you."

That one got me and I nodded, swallowing down the emotions tingling in my eyes and throat.

David had done a complete turnaround since he proposed to me. He'd cut back on his travel, hired a dozen assistants to help him decrease his work load, and now did little more than design the shoes he loved so much.

Jack and he were closer than ever, as were Mum and I. More relationships had been healed in the past year than just ours.

We rounded the corner and stepped through the lounge room. I could hear the muted conversations of the crowd, underlain by soft music playing in the background.

I didn't know what song it was, and I didn't care. I only wanted the man at the end of the aisle to say yes when the celebrant asked him that one important question.

The glass doors through the kitchen to outside were open, and as Jack and I stepped through, the guests stood and turned.

I inhaled sharply, all eyes on me as Jack led me, one step at a time, up a red carpeted aisle.

My heart sung as my eyes met David's, all the love I'd ever hoped for shining in his gaze.

In his arms, was the other love of my life, our smiling, gorgeous little girl.

Victoria.

We stopped and I couldn't help the smile that spread across my face as I gazed at my husband-to-be.

Jack lifted my veil and kissed my cheek, and then I turned to David.

My mother came over to take her beloved granddaughter into her arms and Victoria bounced happily in her granny's arms.

Our daughter loved nothing more than time with her grandparents, and lazy strolls around the orchards.

The celebrant stepped forward and softly said. "Take each other's hands."

We did and she began the service that would bind us for life.

"Dearly beloved. We are gathered here today to join this scientist, and this teacher."

The crowd burst into surprised giggles and so it went on.

Our life would begin anew today as David and I took the next step in our relationship. A promise fulfilled and a family completed.

Forever.

# AFTERWORD

Thank you so much for reading this short example of my style of writing and what I love about romance.
The happily ever afters!

All of my works can be found at www.fionamiers.com

You can contact me anytime time at Fiona.miers@gmail.com

Or you can subscribe to my newsletter where I send out once a fortnight newsletter with deals and free books as well as information on my new releases.
https://www.subscribepage.com/z6d1v5

Thank you so much for reading my story and I hope you have a wonderful day/night/sleep!

www.ingramcontent.com/pod-product-compliance
Lightning Source LLC
Chambersburg PA
CBHW060805210726
48292CB00013B/1841